BISON FRONTIERS OF IMAGINATION

The Absolute at Large

Karel Čapek

INTRODUCTION TO THE BISON BOOKS EDITION BY
Stephen Baxter

University of Nebraska Press
Lincoln and London

Introduction © 2005 by the Board of Regents of the University
of Nebraska
Manufactured in the United States of America

⊗

First Nebraska paperback printing: 2005

Library of Congress Cataloging-in-Publication Data
Capek, Karel, 1890–1938.
[Továrna na absolutno. English]
The absolute at large / Karel Capek; introduction by Stephen
Baxter.
p.   cm.—(Bison frontiers of imagination)
ISBN-13: 978-0-8032-6459-5 (pbk.: alk. paper)
ISBN-10: 0-8032-6459-3 (pbk.: alk. paper)
I. Title.   II. Series.
PG5038.C3T613   2005
891.8'6352—dc22   2005041874

INTRODUCTION

STEPHEN BAXTER

I first read *The Absolute at Large* by Czech writer Karel Čapek when I was sixteen. Knowing nothing of its context, it struck me then as a hilarious example of a brand of science fiction known as a "gadget story," in which the lives of the characters are perturbed by some marvelous new bit of technology. What was remarkable about *Absolute* is that the gadget in question is God. . . . Reading *Absolute* again now, I was struck by how competent it is as a piece of science fiction, how relevant its satirical points remain—and, once again, how funny it is.

Čapek, born 1890, was a writer of novels, stories, and essays on a wide variety of subjects ranging from travel to philosophy. He was active politically and became a close acquaintance of the Czech president. His first works of science fiction were plays, the most notable being *RUR: Rossum's Universal Robots* (1920), which introduced the word "robot" to the world. (The term, actually coined by Čapek's brother and sometime-collaborator Josef, is based on a Slav root meaning "serf labour.") *RUR* foreshadows Čapek's concerns; his robots are metaphors for a world dehumanized by social organization and technology.

The Absolute at Large, published in 1922, was Čapek's first novel. Its original Czech title, *Továrna na Absolutno*, means "The Factory for the Absolute." The story is set in a then-futuristic Czechoslovakia of 1943 (as remote as 2026 is to us). G. H. Bondy, the head of the Metallo-Electric Company, is approached by an engineer, Rudy Marek, who has invented a remarkable new energy source he calls the Karburator. As in all the best hard science fiction the central idea is extrapolated solidly from reality—Čapek was a keen follower of science and was well aware of Ernest Rutherford's discovery of the nucleus in 1911 and his experiments in atom-splitting—and will be familiar to readers today, for the Karburator is an atomic generator, producing energy through the annihilation of matter, just like our modern fission reactors. (Čapek got the date about right; in the real world stable atomic fission was not to be achieved for another two decades.)

But there's a catch in Čapek's story. Everything material is made up of two components, dead matter and the divine—the Absolute. Čapek quotes philosophers like Benedict de Spinoza and Gottfried W. Leibniz to justify this. So if you annihilate the material component you release the Absolute into the world. Whereas Christ and other prophets released the divine by psychic power, the Karburator allowed it to be done mechanically. Marek is aware of this unfortunate byproduct even before he brings the invention to Bondy. But Karburator power is too good of a break to pass up, and the partners go ahead into mass-production and hang the consequences.

Introduction

To develop a good science fiction story you start with a strong core idea, a bit of "what if?" speculation, and then follow through the logical consequences of your premise. And so things develop in *Absolute*. As the roll-out of Karburators to applications like cars and ships and flying machines begins, so the Absolute seeps out, and pockets of religious fervor mushroom. Soon there are rival sects growing around Karburators in ships and fairground rides. Religious disputes break out, for, like the blind men each fingering a different bit of the elephant, each sect, new and old, believes its piece of the Absolute is the only true god.

Not only that, the Absolute infests machines too. Like a technological update of the miracle of the loaves and fishes, factories produce goods in unlimited abundance—and people, bemused by the Absolute, give away their goods, regardless of profit. This leads immediately to an economic crash, for a limitless supply of a product reduces its value to zero. This is a novel by an intelligent man; Čapek's economics are as sound as his scientific and religious understandings, and here he mocks "mystical Communism" (p. 134).

But all of these conflicts escalate. The novel opens out into a multiple-viewpoint disaster story as the world is engulfed by the "Greatest War," which endures to 1953 (chapter XXV). This is still comic, but the comedy is frenetic, edgy, and often very bleak. In the end, with mankind exhausted, the story closes as it opened on a handful of people, and a perhaps too blunt statement of the moral that we must believe in our fellow humans, not just our gods: "We'll kill men, but we want to save mankind. . . . The world will be an evil place as long as people don't believe in other people" (p. 241).

As a piece of comic science fiction, *Absolute* recalls works such as H. G. Wells's "The Man Who Could Work Miracles" (1898), another tale of how the unleashed miraculous could wreck the world, and perhaps Wells's *Food of the Gods* (1904), a fable of economic dislocation. (Čapek had read Wells.) And it foreshadows the works of genre writers like Robert Sheckley in their technological and satirical updating of religious and fairy-tale tropes. In Sheckley's "Something for Nothing" (1953), for instance, a Utiliser is a mechanical genie that gives you anything you want—which is fine until the bill arrives ("122 Dancing Girls . . . 122 million credits"). Perhaps there is even a hint of Douglas Adams in *Absolute*'s frenetically dark comedy.

Of course *Absolute* is a satire, and many of its themes strike chords today. At one level it reads as a prescient fable of atomic power, with its unfulfilled promises of plenty and its dreadful by-products. Bondy and Marek are technocrats driven by dreams of profit to roll out their Karburators even though they know in advance the damage they are likely to cause—just as we, perhaps, keep on burning up the Earth even though we know the harm we are doing. And just as the fictional Marek uncovered the Absolute within matter, perhaps some scientists today are too ready to act as a new priesthood by namedropping God: the Higgs boson is the "God Particle," the patterns of cosmic background radiation are the "Face of God," and so on. Even Einstein proclaimed of quantum mechanics that "God does not play dice" (Einstein's critics asked him how he knew).

And of course Čapek's vision of a world engulfed by a fatal juncture of technology, bigotry, and intolerance has deep resonance for our times.

The best satires endure because they expose deep currents in human nature, transcending their own times. We can enjoy Jonathan Swift's *Gulliver's Travels* (1726) without needing to know anything of Swift's eighteenth-century Britain. Similarly you can, and perhaps should, read *Absolute* without considering its context. But it is very much a novel of its time.

When *Absolute* was published Čapek's Czechoslovakia was only three years old. Čapek's homeland, at the heart of Europe, lay at the junction of cross-continental trade routes and was the product of a collision of traditions and influences. In the sixteenth century ancient nations had been welded into the precarious unity of the Austro-Hungarian Empire. When this empire broke up after the First World War (Čapek was spared enlistment because of health problems with his back), Czechoslovakia was carved out of the empire's remnants. In this young country a thriving community of science fiction writers developed stories of technological and social extrapolation.

But the political situation was unstable. Čapek's Czechoslovakia was sandwiched between a Germany struggling to recover from the war and a coalescing Soviet system in Russia. It's no surprise that *Absolute* pictures the world as a fragile place full of precarious institutions ready to be overwhelmed by rampant ideologies. As science fiction writers go Čapek was no prophet despite the robots and the atomic reactors: *Absolute* depicts a 1943 in which Russia is run by the Tsars once more and China is ruled by "mandarins." But his fragile and edgy comedy caught the currents of his times on a deeper, metaphorical level. His last novel, *The War with the Newts*, a dark tale of deep-sea aliens seeking *lebensraum*, was published in 1936 when Hitler was already drawing up his plans for the dismemberment of Čapek's young country.

The Munich settlement of 1938, which allowed the Nazis to overrun Czechoslovakia, was a bitter blow to Čapek, who had been an ardent and loud opponent of fascism. Čapek would have been one of the Nazis' first targets, and he was given offers of refuge in the west. But his health rapidly deteriorated; he died of pneumonia in Prague on December 25, 1938. The Nazis blacklisted his works and sent his brother Josef to Belsen, where he died. Perhaps it is well Čapek did not live to see this.

Čapek was perhaps a humanist and a humorist. As a humanist he believed a just world order could only be built on the respect of one person for another. In *Absolute* Čapek's targets were not science, business, religion, or politics in themselves but absolutism in any of these realms at the expense of humanity. As a humorist, he expressed these ideas through his dystopian fables of what happens if you give way to opposite tendencies—and his warnings were borne out. In Prague the anniversary of his death is commemorated each Christmas Day.

The Absolute at Large is good science fiction, a fine piece of comic writing, an enduring satire on aspects of our human nature, and a cry of defiant mockery from a dark time in our history. It deserves to be read, and I'm delighted that the University of Nebraska Press has brought it back into print.

CONTENTS

Contents

THE ABSOLUTE AT LARGE

THE ABSOLUTE AT LARGE

CHAPTER I

THE ADVERTISEMENT

O<small>N</small> New Year's Day, 1943, C. H. Bondy, head of the great Metallo-Electric Company, was sitting as usual reading his paper. He skipped the news from the theatre of war rather disrespectfully, avoided the Cabinet crisis, then crowded on sail (for the *People's Journal,* which had grown long ago to five times its ancient size, now afforded enough canvas for an ocean voyage) for the Finance and Commerce section. Here he cruised about for quite a while, then furled his sails, and abandoned himself to his thoughts.

"The Coal Crisis!" he said to himself. "Mines getting worked out; the Ostrava basin suspending work for years. Heavens above, it's a sheer disaster! We'll have to import Upper Silesian coal. Just work out what that will add to the cost of our manufacturers, and then talk about competition. We're in a pretty fix. And if Germany raises her tariff, we may as well shut up shop. And the Industrial Banks going down, too! What a wretched state of affairs!

What a hopeless, stupid, stifling state of affairs!
Oh, damn the crisis!"

Here G. H. Bondy, Chairman of the Board of
Directors, came to a pause. Something was fidget-
ing him and would not let him rest. He traced it
back to the last page of his discarded newspaper. It
was the syllable TION, only part of a word, for the
fold of the paper came just in front of the T. It
was this very incompleteness which had so curiously
impressed itself upon him.

"Well, hang it, it's probably IRON PRODUCTION,"
Bondy pondered vaguely, "or PREVENTION, or,
maybe, RESTITUTION. . . . And the Azote shares have
gone down, too. The stagnation's simply shocking.
The position's so bad that it's ridiculous. . . . But
that's nonsense: who would advertise the RESTITU-
TION of anything? More likely RESIGNATION. It's
sure to be RESIGNATION."

With a touch of annoyance, G. H. Bondy spread
out the newspaper to dispose of this irritating word.
It had now vanished amid the chequering of the
small advertisements. He hunted for it from one
column to another, but it had concealed itself with
provoking ingenuity. Mr. Bondy then worked from
the bottom up, and finally started again from the
right-hand side of the page. The contumacious
"tion" was not to be found.

Mr. Bondy did not give in. He refolded the

paper along its former creases, and behold, the detestable TION leaped forth on the very edge. Keeping his finger firmly on the spot, he swiftly spread the paper out once more, and found—— Mr. Bondy swore under his breath. It was nothing but a very modest, very commonplace small advertisement:

INVENTION.

Highly remunerative, suitable for any factory, for immediate sale, personal reasons. Apply R. Marek, Engineer, Břevnov, 1651.

"So that's all it was!" thought G. H. Bondy. "Some sort of patent braces; just a cheap swindle or some crazy fellow's pet plaything. And here I've wasted five minutes on it! I'm getting scatterbrained myself. What a wretched state of affairs! And not a hint of improvement anywhere!"

He settled himself in a rocking-chair to savour in more comfort the full bitterness of this wretched state of affairs. True, the M.E.C. had ten factories and 34,000 employees. The M.E.C. was the leading producer of iron. The M.E.C. had no competitor as regards boilers. The M.E.C. grates were world-famous. But after thirty years' hard work, gracious Heavens, surely one would have got bigger results elsewhere. . . . .

G. H. Bondy sat up with a jerk. "R. Marek, Engineer; R. Marek, Engineer. Half a minute:

mightn't that be that red-haired Marek—let's see, what was his name? Rudolph, Rudy Marek, my old chum Rudy of the Technical School? Sure enough, here it is in the advertisement: 'R. Marek, Engineer.' Rudy, you rascal, is it possible? Well, you've not got on very far in the world, my poor fellow! Selling 'a highly remunerative invention.' Ha! ha! '. . . for personal reasons.' We know all about those 'personal reasons.' No money, isn't that what it is? You want to catch some jay of a manufacturer on a nicely limed 'patent,' do you? Oh, well, you always had rather a notion of turning the world upside down. Ah, my lad, where are all our fine notions now! And those extravagant, romantic days when we were young!"

Bondy lay back in his chair once more.

"It's quite likely it really is Marek," he reflected. "Still, Marek had a head for science. He was a bit of a talker, but there was a touch of genius about the lad. He had ideas. In other respects he was a fearfully unpractical fellow. An absolute fool, in fact. It's very surprising that he isn't a Professor," mused Mr. Bondy. "I haven't set eyes on him for twenty years. God knows what he has been up to; perhaps he's come right down in the world. Yes, he must be down and out, living away over in Břevnov, poor chap . . . and getting a living out of inventions! What an awful finish!"

He tried to imagine the straits of the fallen inventor. He managed to picture a horribly shaggy and dishevelled head, surrounded by dismal paper walls like those in a film. There is no furniture, only a mattress in the corner, and a pitiful model made of spools, nails, and match-ends on the table. A murky window looks out on a little yard. Upon this scene of unspeakable indigence enters a visitor in rich furs. "I have come to have a look at your invention." The half-blind inventor fails to recognize his old schoolfellow. He humbly bows his tousled head, looks about for a seat to offer to his guest, and then, oh Heaven! with his poor, stiff, shaking fingers he tries to get his sorry invention going— it's some crazy perpetual motion device—and mumbles confusedly that it should work, and certainly *would* work, if only he had . . . if only he could buy. . . . The fur-coated visitor looks all around the garret, and suddenly he takes a leather wallet from his pocket and lays on the table one, two (Mr. Bondy takes fright and cries "That's enough!") three thousand-crown notes. ("One would have been quite enough . . . to go on with, I mean," protests something in Mr. Bondy's brain.)

"There is . . . something to carry on the work with, Mr. Marek. No, no, you're not in any way indebted to me. Who am I? That doesn't matter. Just take it that I am a friend."

Bondy, found this scene very pleasant and touch-ing.

"I'll send my secretary to Marek," he resolved; "to-morrow without fail. And what shall I do to-day? It's a holiday; I'm not going to the works. My time's my own . . . a wretched state things are in! Nothing to do all day long! Suppose I went round to-day myself."

G. H. Bondy hesitated. It would be a bit of an adventure to go and see for oneself how that queer fellow was struggling along in Břevnov.

"After all, we were such chums! And old times have their claim on one. Yes, I'll go!" decided Mr. Bondy. And he went.

He had rather a boring time while his car was gliding all over Břevnov in search of a mean hovel bearing the number 1651. They had to inquire at the police-station.

"Marek, Marek," said the inspector, searching his memory. "That must be Marek the engineer, of Marek and Co., the electric lamp factory, 1651, Mixa Street."

The electric lamp factory! Bondy felt disap-pointed, even annoyed. Rudy Marek wasn't living up in a garret, then! He was a manufacturer and wanted to sell some invention or other "for personal reasons." If that didn't smell of bankruptcy, his name wasn't Bondy.

"Do you happen to know how Mr. Marek is doing?" he asked the police inspector, with a casual air, as he took his seat in the car.

"Oh, splendidly!" the inspector answered. "He's got a very fine business." Local pride made him add, "The firm's very well known"; and he amplified this with: "A very wealthy man, and a learned one, too. He does nothing but make experiments."

"Mixa Street!" cried Bondy to his chauffeur.

"Third on the right!" the inspector called after the car.

Bondy was soon ringing at the residential part of quite a pretty little factory.

"It's all very nice and clean here," he remarked to himself. "Flower-beds in the yard, creeper on the walls. Humph! There always was a touch of the philanthropist and reformer about that confounded Marek." And at that moment Marek himself came out on the steps to meet him; Rudy Marek, awfully thin and serious-looking, up in the clouds, so to speak. It gave Bondy a queer pang to find him neither so young as he used to be nor so unkempt as that inventor; so utterly different from what Bondy had imagined that he was scarcely recognizable. But before he could fully realize his disillusionment, Marek stretched out his hand and said quietly, "Well, so you've come at last, Bondy! I've been expecting you!"

CHAPTER II

THE KARBURATOR

"I've been expecting you!" Marek repeated, when he had seated his guest in a comfortable leather chair. Nothing on earth would have induced Bondy to own up to his vision of the fallen inventor. "Just fancy!" he said, with a rather forced gaiety. "What a coincidence! It struck me only this very morning that we hadn't seen one another for twenty years. Twenty years, Rudy, think of it!"

"Hm," said Marek. "And so you want to buy my invention."

"Buy it?" said G. H. Bondy hesitatingly. "I really don't know . . . I haven't even given it a thought. I wanted to see you and——"

"Oh, come, you needn't pretend," Marek interrupted him. "I knew that you were coming. You'd be sure to, for a thing like this. This kind of invention is just in your line. There's a lot to be done with it." He made an eloquent motion with his hand, coughed, and began again more deliberately. "The invention I am going to show you means a bigger revolution in technical methods than Watt's

8

invention of the steam-engine. To give you its nature briefly, it provides, putting it theoretically, for the *complete utilization of atomic energy.*"

Bondy concealed a yawn. "But tell me, what have you been doing all these twenty years?"

Marek glanced at him with some surprise.

"Modern science teaches that all matter—that is to say, its atoms—is composed of a vast number of units of energy. An atom is in reality a collection of electrons, *i.e.* of the tiniest particles of electricity."

"That's tremendously interesting," Bondy broke in. "I was always weak in physics, you know. But you're not looking well, Marek. By the way, how did you happen to come by this playth . . . this, er . . . factory?"

"I? Oh, quite by accident. I invented a new kind of filament for electric bulbs. . . . But that's nothing; I only came upon it incidentally. You see, for twenty years I've been working on the combustion of matter. Tell me yourself, Bondy, what is the greatest problem of modern industry?"

"Doing business," said Bondy. "And are you married yet?"

"I'm a widower," answered Marek, leaping up excitedly. "No, business has nothing to do with it, I tell you. It's combustion. The complete utilization of the heat-energy contained in matter! Just consider that we use hardly one hundred-thousandth of the heat that there is in coal, and that could be extracted from it! Do you realize that!"

"Yes, coal is terribly dear!" said Mr. Bondy sapiently.

Marek sat down and cried disgustedly, "Look here, if you haven't come here about my Karburator, Bondy, you can go."

"Go ahead, then," Bondy returned, anxious to conciliate him.

Marek rested his head in his hands, and after a struggle came out with, "For twenty years I've been working on it, and now—now, I'll sell it to the first man who comes along! My magnificent dream! The greatest invention of all the ages! Seriously, Bondy, I tell you, it's something really amazing."

"No doubt, in the present wretched state of affairs," assented Bondy.

"No, without any qualification at all, amazing. Do you realize that it means the utilization of atomic energy without any residue whatever?"

"Aha," said Bondy. "So we're going to do our heating with atoms. Well, why not? . . . You've got a nice place here, Rudy. Small and pleasant. How many hands do you employ?"

Marek took no notice. "You know," he said thoughtfully, "it's all the same thing, whatever you call it—the utilization of atomic energy, or the complete combustion of matter, or the disintegration of matter. You can call it what you please."

"I'm in favour of 'combustion'!" said Mr. Bondy. "It sounds more familiar."

"But 'disintegration' is more exact—to break up the atoms into electrons, and harness the electrons and make them work. Do you understand that?"

"Perfectly," Bondy assured him. "The point is to harness them!"

"Well, imagine, say, that there are two horses at the ends of a rope, pulling with all their might in opposite directions. Do you know what you have then?"

"Some kind of sport, I suppose," suggested Mr. Bondy.

"No, a state of repose. The horses pull, but they stay where they are. And if you were to cut the rope——"

"—The horses would fall over," cried G. H. Bondy, with a flash of inspiration.

"No, but they would start running; they would become energy released. Now, pay attention. Matter is a team in that very position. Cut the bonds that hold its electrons together, and they will . . ."

"Run loose!"

"Yes, but we can catch and harness them, don't you see? Or put it to yourself this way: we burn a piece of coal, say, to produce heat. We do get a little heat from it, but we also get ashes, coal-gas, and soot. So we don't lose the matter altogether, do we?"

"No.—Won't you have a cigar?"

"No, I won't.—But the matter which is left still contains a vast quantity of unused atomic energy. If we used up the whole of the atomic energy, we should use up the whole of the atoms. In short, *the matter would vanish altogether.*"

"Aha! Now I understand."

"It's just as though we were to grind corn badly —as if we ground up the thin outer husk and threw the rest away, just as we throw away ashes. When the grinding is perfect, there's nothing or next to nothing left of the grain, is there? In the same way, when there is perfect combustion, there's nothing or next to nothing left of the matter we burn. It's ground up completely. It is used up. It returns to its original nothingness. You know, it takes a tremendous amount of energy to make matter exist at all. Take away its existence, compel it not to be, and you thereby release an enormous supply of power. That's how it is, Bondy."

"Aha. That's not bad."

"Pflüger, for instance, calculates that one kilogramme of coal contains twenty-three billions of calories. I think that Pflüger exaggerates."

"Decidedly."

"I have arrived at seven billions myself, theoretically. But even that signifies that one kilogramme of coal, if it underwent complete combustion, would run a good-sized factory for several hundred hours!"

"The devil it does!" cried Mr. Bondy, springing from his chair.

"I can't give you the exact number of hours. I've been burning half a kilogramme of coal for six weeks at a pressure of thirty kilogrammetres and, man alive," said the engineer in a whisper, turning pale, "it's still going on . . . and on . . . and on."

Bondy was embarrassed; he stroked his smooth round chin. "Listen, Marek," he began, hesitatingly. "You're surely . . . er . . . a bit . . . er . . . overworked."

Marek's hand thrust the suggestion aside. "Not a bit of it. If you'd only get up physics a bit, I could give you an explanation of my Karburator [1] in which the combustion takes place. It involves a whole chapter of advanced physics, you know. But you'll see it downstairs in the cellar. I shovelled half a kilogramme of coal into the machine, then I shut it up and had it officially sealed in the presence

[1] This name which Marek gave to his atomic boiler is, of course, quite incorrect, and is one of the melancholy results of the ignorance of Latin among technicians. A more exact term would have been Komburator, Atomic Kettle, Karbowatt, Disintegrator, Motor M, Bondymover, Hylergon, Molecular Disintegration Dynamo, E. W., and other designations which were later proposed. It was, of course, the bad one that was generally adopted.

of witnesses, so that no one could put any more coal in. Go and have a look at it for yourself—go on— go now! You won't understand it, anyway, but— go down to the cellar! Go on down, man, I tell you!"

"Won't you come with me?" asked Bondy in astonishment.

"No, you go alone. And . . . I say, Bondy . . . don't stay down there long."

"Why not?" asked Bondy, growing a trifle suspicious.

"Oh, nothing much. Only I've a notion that perhaps it's not quite healthy down there. Turn on the light, the switch is just by the door. That noise down in the cellar doesn't come from my machine. It works noiselessly, steadily, and without any smell. . . . The roaring is only a . . . a ventilator. Well, now, you go on. I'll wait here. Then you can tell me . . ."

*   *   *   *   *

Bondy went down the cellar steps, quite glad to be away from that madman for a while (quite mad, no doubt whatever about it) and rather worried as to the quickest means of getting out of the place altogether. Why, just look, the cellar had a huge thick reinforced door just like an armour-plated safe in a bank. And now let's have a light. The switch was just by the door. And there in the middle of the arched concrete cellar, clean as a monastery cell, lay a gigantic copper cylinder resting on cement supports. It was closed on all sides except at the top, where there was a grating bedecked with seals. Inside the machine all was darkness and silence. With a smooth and regular motion the cylinder thrust forth a piston which slowly rotated a heavy fly-wheel. That was all. Only the ventilator in the cellar window kept up a ceaseless rattle.

Perhaps it was the draught from the ventilator or something—but Mr. Bondy felt a peculiar breeze upon his brow, and an eerie sensation as though his hair were standing on end; and then it seemed as if he were being borne through boundless space; and then as though he were floating in the air without any sensation of his own weight. G. H. Bondy fell on his knees, lost in a bewildering, shining ecstasy. He felt as if he must shout and sing, he seemed to hear about him the rustle of unceasing and innumerable wings. And suddenly someone seized him violently by the hand and dragged him from the cellar. It was Marek, wearing over his head a mask or a helmet like a diver's, and he hauled Bondy up the stairs.

Up in the room he pulled off his metal head-covering and wiped away the sweat that soaked his brow.

"Only just in time," he gasped, showing tremendous agitation.

CHAPTER III

G. H. BONDY felt rather as though he were dreaming. Marek settled him in an easy chair with quite maternal solicitude, and made haste to bring some brandy.

"Here, drink this up quickly," he jerked out hoarsely, offering him the glass with a trembling hand. "*You* came over queer down there too, didn't you?"

"On the contrary," Bondy answered unsteadily. "It was . . . it was beautiful, old chap! I felt as if I were flying, or something like that."

"Yes, yes," said Marek quickly. "That's exactly what I mean. As though you were flying along, or rather soaring upward, wasn't that it?"

"It was a feeling of perfect bliss," said Mr. Bondy. "I think it's what you'd call being transported. As if there was something down there . . . something . . ."

"Something—holy?" asked Marek hesitatingly.

"Perhaps. Yes, man alive, you're right. I never go to church, Rudy, never in my life, but down in

16

that cellar I felt as if I were in church. Tell me, man, what did I do down there?"

"You went on your knees," Marek muttered with a bitter smile, and began striding up and down the room.

Bondy stroked his bald head in bewilderment.

"That's extraordinary. But come, on my knees? Well, then, tell me what . . . what is there in the cellar that acts on one so queerly?"

"The Karburator," growled Marek, gnawing his lips. His cheeks seemed even more sunken than before, and were as pale as death.

"But, confound it, man," cried Bondy in amazement, "how can it be?"

The engineer only shrugged his shoulders, and with bent head went on pacing up and down the room.

G. H. Bondy's eyes followed him with childish astonishment. "The man's crazy," he said to himself. "All the same, what the devil is it that comes over one in that cellar? That tormenting bliss, that tremendous security, that terror, that overwhelming feeling of devotion, or whatever you like to call it." Mr. Bondy arose and poured himself out another dash of brandy.

"I say, Marek," he said, "I've got it now."

"Got what?" exclaimed Marek, halting.

"That business in the cellar. That queer psychical condition. It's some form of poisoning, isn't it? . . ."

Marek gave an angry laugh. "Oh, yes, of course, poisoning!"

"I thought so at once," declared Bondy, his mind at rest in an instant. "That apparatus of yours produces something, ah . . . er . . . something like ozone, doesn't it? Or more likely poisonous gas. And when anyone inhales it, it . . . er . . . poisons him or excites him somehow, isn't that it? Why, of course, man, it's nothing but poisonous gases; they're probably given off somehow by the combustion of the coal in that . . . that Karburator of yours. Some sort of illuminating gas or paradise gas, or phosgene or something of the sort. That's why you've put in the ventilator, and that's why you wear a gas-mask when you go into the cellar, isn't it? Just some confounded gases."

"If only there were nothing but *gases!*" Marek burst out, shaking his fists threateningly. "Look here, Bondy, that's why I must sell that Karburator! I simply can't stand it—I can't stand it . . . *I can't stand it,*" he shouted, well-nigh weeping. "I never dreamed my Karburator would do anything like *this* . . . this . . . terrifying mischief! Just think, it's been going on like *that* from the very beginning! And every one feels it who comes near the thing. You haven't any notion even yet, Bondy. But our porter caught it properly."

"Poor fellow!" said the astonished Bondy, full of sympathy. "And did he die of it?"

"No, but he got *converted*," cried Marek in despair. "Bondy, you're a man I can confide in. My invention, my Karburator, has one terrible defect. Nevertheless, you're going to buy it or else take it from me as a gift. You will, Bondy—even if it spews forth demons. It doesn't matter to you, Bondy, so long as you can get your millions out of it. And you'll get them, man. It's a stupendous thing, I tell you——; but I don't want to have anything more to do with it. You haven't such a sensitive conscience as I have, you know, Bondy. It'll bring in millions, thousands of millions; but it will lay a frightful load upon your conscience. Make up your mind!"

"Oh, leave me alone," Mr. Bondy protested. "If it gives off poisonous gases, the authorities will prohibit it, and there's an end of it. You know the wretched state of affairs here. Now in America . . ."

"It isn't poisonous gases," Marek exclaimed. "It's *something a thousand times worse*. Mark what I tell you, Bondy, it's something beyond human reason, but there's not a scrap of deception about it. Well, then, my Karburator actually does burn up matter, causes its utter combustion, so that not even a grain of dust remains. Or rather, it breaks it up, crushes it, splits it up into electrons, consumes it, grinds it—I don't know how to express it—in short, uses it up completely. You have no idea what a colossal amount of energy is contained in the atoms. With half a hundredweight of coal in the Karbura-ator you can sail right round the world in a steam-ship, you can light the whole city of Prague, you can supply power for the whole of a huge factory, or anything you like. A bit of coal the size of a nut will do the heating and the cooking for a whole family. And ultimately we shan't even require coal; we can do our heating with the first pebble or hand-ful of dirt we pick up in front of the house. Every scrap of matter has in it more energy than an enor-mous boiler; you've only to extract it. You've only to know how to secure total combustion! Well, Bondy, I can do it; my Karburator can do it. You'll admit, Bondy, that it has been worth while toiling over it for twenty years."

"Look here, Rudy," Bondy began slowly, "it's all very extraordinary—but I believe you, so to speak. On my soul, I do believe you. You know, when I stood in front of that Karburator of yours, I felt that I was in the presence of something over-poweringly great, something a man could not with-stand. I can't help it: I believe you. Down there in the cellar you have something uncanny, some-thing that will overturn the whole world."

"Alas, Bondy," Marek whispered anxiously,

"that's just where the trouble is. Listen, and I'll tell you the whole thing. Have you ever read Spinoza?"

"No."

"No more had I. But now, you see, I am beginning to read that sort of thing. I don't understand it—it's terribly difficult stuff for us technical people —but there's something in it. Do you by any chance believe in God?"

"I? Well, now . . ." G. H. Bondy deliberated. "Upon my word, I couldn't say. Perhaps there is a God, but He's on some other planet. Not on ours. Oh, well, that sort of thing doesn't fit in with our times at all. Tell me, what makes you drag that into it?"

"I don't believe in anything," said Marek in a hard voice. "I don't want to believe. I have always been an atheist. I believed in matter and in progress and in nothing else. I'm a scientific man, Bondy; and science cannot admit the existence of God."

"From the business point of view," Mr. Bondy remarked, "it's a matter of indifference. If He wants to exist, in Heaven's name, let Him. We aren't mutually exclusive."

"But from the scientific point of view, Bondy," cried the engineer sternly, "it is absolutely intolerable. It's a case of Him or science. I don't as-

sert that God does not exist; I only assert that He
ought not to exist, or at least ought not to let Himself be seen. And I believe that science is crowding
Him out step by step, or at any rate is preventing
Him from letting Himself be seen; and I believe
that that is the greatest mission of science."

"Possibly," said Bondy calmly. "But go on."

"And now just imagine, Bondy, that—— But
wait, I'll put it to you this way. Do you know what
Pantheism is? It's the belief that God, or the Absolute, if you prefer it, is manifest in everything that
exists. In men, as in stones, in the grass, the water
—everywhere. And do you know what Spinoza
teaches? That matter is only the outward manifestation, only one phase of the divine substance, the
other phase of which is spirit. And do you know
what Fechner teaches?"

"No, I don't," the other admitted.

"Fechner teaches that everything, everything that
is, is penetrated with the divine, that God fills with
His being the whole of the matter in the world. And
do you know Leibniz? Leibniz teaches that physical matter is composed of psychical atoms, monads,
whose nature is divine. What do you say to that?"

"I don't know," said G. H. Bondy. "I don't understand it."

"Nor do I. It's fearfully abstruse. But let us
assume, for the sake of argument, that God is con-

tained in all forms of physical matter, that He is, as it were, imprisoned in it. And when you smash this matter up completely, He flies out of it as though from a box. He is suddenly set free. He is released from matter as illuminating gas is from coal. You have only to burn one single atom up completely, and immediately the whole cellar is filled with the Absolute. It's simply appalling how quickly it spreads."

"Hold on," Mr. Bondy interrupted. "Say that all over again, but say it slowly."

"Look at it like this then," said Marek. "We're assuming that all matter contains the Absolute in some state of confinement. We can call it a latent imprisoned force, or simply say that as God is omnipresent He is therefore present in all matter and in every particle of matter. And now suppose you utterly destroy a piece of matter, apparently leaving not the slightest residue. Then, since all matter is really Matter plus Absolute, what you have destroyed is *only* the matter, and you're left with an indestructible residue—free and active Absolute. You're left with the chemically unanalysable, immaterial residue, which shows no spectrum lines, neither atomic weight nor chemical affinity, no obedience to Boyle's law, none, none whatever, of the properties of matter. What is left behind is pure God. A chemical nullity which acts with monstrous energy. Being immaterial, it is not subject to the laws of matter. Thence, it already follows that its manifestations are contrary to nature and downright miraculous. All this proceeds from the assumption that God is present in all matter. Can you imagine, for the sake of argument, that He is really so present?"

"I certainly can," said Bondy. "What then?"

"Good," said Marek, rising to his feet. "Then *it's the solemn truth.*"

CHAPTER IV

GOD IN THE CELLAR

G. H. BONDY sucked meditatively at his cigar. "And how did you find it out, old chap?" he asked at last.

"By the effect on myself," said the engineer, resuming his march up and down the room. "As a result of its complete disintegration of matter, my Perfect Karburator manufactures a by-product: pure and unconfined Absolute, God in a chemically pure form. At one end, so to speak, it emits mechanical power, and at the other, the divine principle. Just as when you split water up into hydrogen and oxygen, only on an immensely larger scale."

"Hm," said Mr. Bondy. "And then—?"

"I've an idea," continued Marek cautiously, "that there are many of the elect who can separate the material substance in themselves from the divine substance. They can release or distil the Absolute, as it were, from their material selves. Christ and the miracle-workers, fakirs, mediums, and prophets have achieved it by means of their psychic power.

My Karburator does it by a purely mechanical process. It acts, you might say, as a factory for the Absolute."

"Facts," said G. H. Bondy. "Stick to facts."

"These are facts. I constructed my Perfect Karburator only in theory to begin with. Then I made a little model, which wouldn't go. The fourth model was the first that really worked. It was only about so big, but it ran quite nicely. But even while I was working with it on this small scale, I felt peculiar physical effects—a strange exhilaration—a 'fey' feeling. But I thought it was due to being so pleased about the invention, or to being overworked, perhaps. It was then that I first began to prophesy and perform miracles."

"To do *what?*" Bondy cried.

"To prophesy and perform miracles," Marek repeated gloomily. "I had moments of astounding illumination. I saw, for instance, quite clearly, things that would happen in the future. I predicted even your visit here. And once I tore my nail off on a lathe. I looked at the damaged finger, and all at once a new nail grew on it. Very likely I'd formed the wish, but all the same it's queer and . . . terrible. Another time—just think of it—I rose right up into the air. It's called levitation, you know. I never believed in any rubbish of that kind, so you can imagine the shock it gave me."

"I can quite believe it," said Bondy gravely. "It must be most distressing."

"Extremely distressing. I thought it must be due to nerves, a kind of auto-suggestion or something. In the meanwhile I erected the big Karburator in the cellar and started it off. As I told you, it's been running now for six weeks, day and night. And it was there that I first realized the full significance of the business. In a single day the cellar was chock-full of the Absolute, ready to burst with it; and it began to spread all over the house. The pure Absolute pentrates all matter, you know, but it takes a little longer with solid substances. In the air it spread as swiftly as light. When I went in, I tell you, man, it took me like a stroke. I shrieked out aloud. I don't know where I got the strength to run away. When I got upstairs, I thought over the whole business. My first notion was that it must be some new intoxicating, stimulating gas, developed by the process of complete combustion. That's why I had that ventilator fixed up, from the outside. Two of the fitters on the job "saw the light" and had visions; the third was a drinker and so perhaps to some extent immune. As long as I thought it was only a gas, I made a series of experiments with it, and it's interesting to find that any light burns much more brightly in the Absolute. If it would let itself be confined in glass bulbs, I'd fill lamps with it; but it escapes from any vessel, however thick you make it. Then I decided it must be some sort of Ultra-X-ray, but there's no tràce of any form of electricity, and it makes no impression on photo-sensitive plates. On the third day, the porter and his wife, who live just over the cellar, had to be taken off to the sanatorium."

"What for?" asked Bondy.

"He got religion. He was inspired. He gave religious addresses and performed miracles. His wife uttered prophecies. My porter had been a thoroughly hard-headed chap, a monist and a freethinker, and an unusually steady fellow. Well, just fancy, from no visible cause whatever, he started healing people by laying on of hands. Of course, Bondy, he was reported at once. The district health officer, who is a friend of mine, was tremendously upset about it; so, to avoid any scandal, I had the porter sent to a sanatorium. They say he's better now; quite cured. He has lost the power to perform miracles. I'm going to send him on the land to recuperate. . . . Then I began to work miracles myself and see into the future. Among other things, I had visions of gigantic, swampy primeval forests, overgrown with mosses and inhabited by weird monsters—probably because the Karburator was burning Upper Silesian coal, which is of the oldest forma-

tion. Possibly the God of the Carboniferous Age
is in it."

Mr. Bondy shuldered. "Marek, this is frightful!"

"It is indeed," said Marek sorrowfully. "Gradually I began to see that it wasn't gas, but the Absolute. The symptoms were terrible. I could read
people's thoughts, light emanated from me, I had a
desperate struggle not to become absorbed in prayer
and preach belief in God. I tried to clog the Karburator up with sand, but I was seized with a bout of
levitation. That machine won't let anything stop it.
I don't sleep at home nowadays. Even in the factory
there have been several serious cases of illumination
among the workmen. I don't know where to turn,
Bondy. Yes, I've tried every possible isolating
material that might prevent the Absolute from getting out of the cellar. Ashes, sand, metal walls,
nothing can keep it back. I've even tried covering
the cellar with the work of Professor Krejči,
Spencer, Haeckel, and all the Positivists you can
think of: would you believe it, the Absolute goes
calmly through even that stuff! Even papers, prayer-
books, Lives of the Saints, Patriotic Song-books,
university lectures, best-sellers, political treatises,
and Parliamentary Reports, present no obstacle to
it. I'm simply desperate. You can't shut it up, you
can't soak it up. It's mischief let loose."

"Oh, but why?" said Mr. Bondy. "Does it really mean such mischief? Even if all this were true . . . is it such a disaster?"

"Bondy, my Karburator is a terrific thing. It will overturn the whole world, mechanically and socially. It will cheapen production to an unbelievable extent. It will do away with poverty and hunger. It will some day save our planet from freezing up. But, on the other hand, it hurls God as a by-product into the world. I implore you, Bondy, don't underrate what it means. We aren't used to reckoning with God as a *reality*. We don't know what His presence may bring about—say, socially, morally, and so on. Why, man, this thing affects the whole of human civilization!"

"Wait a minute!" said Bondy thoughtfully. "Perhaps there's some charm or other that would exorcise it. Have you called in the clergy?"

"What kind of clergy?"

"Any kind. The denomination probably makes no difference in this case, you know. Perhaps they could do something to stop it."

"Oh, that's all superstition!" burst out Marek. "Leave me alone with your parsons! Catch me giving them a chance to make a miraculous shrine out of my cellar! Me, with my views!"

"Very well," declared Mr. Bondy. "Then I'll call them in myself. You never can tell. . . .

Come, it can't do any harm, anyway. After all, I
haven't anything against God. Only He oughtn't
to interfere with business. Have you tried nego-
tiating with Him in a friendly spirit?"

"No," admitted the engineer.

"That was a mistake," said Bondy dryly. "Perhaps you could come to some agreement with Him.
A proper formal contract, in something like this
style: 'We guarantee to produce You discreetly and
continuously to an extent to be fixed by mutual agreement; in return for which You pledge yourself to
refrain from any divine manifestations within such
and such a radius from the place of origin.' What
do you think—would He consider these terms?"

"I don't know," answered Marek uneasily. "He
seems to have a decided inclination in favour of
becoming independent of matter once more. Still,
perhaps . . . in His own interests . . . He
might be willing to listen. But don't ask me to
do it."

"Very well, then!" Bondy agreed. "I'll send my
own solicitor. A very tactful and capable fellow.
And then again . . . er . . . . one might
perhaps offer Him some church or other. After
all, a factory cellar and its surroundings are rather
. . . well . . . undignified quarters for Him.
We ought to ascertain His tastes. Have you tried
yet?"

"No; it would suit me best to flood the cellar with water."

"Gently, Marek, gently. I'm probably going to buy this invention. You understand, of course, that . . . I'll send my experts over first . . . we'll have to look into the business a little further. Perhaps it's only poisonous fumes, after all. And if it actually turns out to be God Himself, that's all right. So long as the Karburator really works."

Marek got up. "And you wouldn't be afraid to install the Karburator in the M.E.C. works?"

"I'm not afraid," said Bondy, rising, "to manufacture Karburators wholesale. Karburators for trains and ships. Karburators for central heating, for houses, offices, factories, and schools. In ten years' time all the heating in the world will be done by Karburators. I'll give you three per cent. of the gross profits. The first year it will only be a few millions, perhaps. Meanwhile you can move out, so that I can send my men along. I'll bring the Suffragan Bishop up to-morrow morning. See that you keep out of his way, Rudy. I don't like seeing you about here in any case. You are rather abrupt, and I don't want to offend the Absolute to start with."

"Bondy," Marek whispered, horror-stricken. "I

warn you for the last time. It means letting God loose upon this world!"

"Then," said G. H. Bondy, with dignity, "He will be personally indebted to me to that extent. And I hope that He won't show me any ill-feeling."

CHAPTER V

Aʙᴏᴜᴛ a fortnight after New Year's Day, Marek was sitting in Bondy's business office.

"How far have you got?" Bondy had just asked, raising his head from some papers over which he was bending.

"I've finished," said the engineer. "I've given your engineers detailed drawings of the Karburator. That bald-headed fellow—what's his name——"

"Krolmus."

"Yes, Krolmus has simplified my atomic motor amazingly—the transformation of electronic energy into motor power, you know. He's an able fellow, my boy, is Krolmus. And what other news is there?"

G. H. Bondy went on writing assiduously.

"We're building," he said after a while. "Seven thousand bricklayers on the job. A factory for Karburators."

"At Vysočany. And we've increased our share capital. A billion and a half. Our new invention's getting into the papers. See for yourself," he added, tipping half a hundredweight of Czech and foreign

34

papers into Marek's lap, then buried himself in the documents on his desk.

"I haven't been for a fortnight," said Marek gloomily.

"Haven't been where?"

"I haven't been to my little factory out at Břevnov for a fortnight. I—I daren't go there. Is anything being done there?"

"Mphm."

"And what about my Karburator?" asked Marek, controlling his anxiety.

"It's still running."

"And what about . . . the other thing?"

The Chief sighed and laid down his pen. "Do you know that we had to have Mixa Street closed?"

"Why?"

"People kept going there to pray. Whole processions of them. The police tried to disperse them, and seven people lost their lives. They let themselves be knocked over like sheep."

"I feared as much, I feared as much," muttered Marek in despair.

"We've blocked the street with barbed wire," Bondy went on. "We had to clear the people out of the neighbouring houses—religious manifestations all over them, you know. A commission of the Ministries of Health and Education is occupying them now."

"I expect," said Marek with a breath of relief, "that the authorities will prohibit my Karburator."

"Oh, no they won't," said G. H. Bondy. "The Clerical party are making a fearful row about your Karburator, and for that very reason the progressive parties have taken it under their wing. In reality no one knows what it's all about. It's evident that you don't read the papers, man. It's developed into a quite needless attack upon clericalism, and the Church happens to have a little right on its side in this case. That confounded Bishop informed the Cardinal Archbishop——"

"What Bishop?"

"Oh, some Bishop by the name of Linda, quite a sensible man in other respects. You see, I took him up *there* as an expert, to inspect the wonder-working Absolute. His inspection lasted a full three hours, and he spent the whole time in the cellar, and . . ."

"He got religion?" burst out Marek.

"Not a bit of it! Perhaps, he's had too long a training with God, or else he's a more hard-baked atheist than you; I don't know. But three days later he came to me and told me that from the Catholic standpoint God cannot be brought into the matter, that the Church absolutely rejects and forbids the pantheistic hypothesis as heresy. In short, that this isn't any legal, duly recognized God, supported by the authority of the Church, and that, as a priest, he must declare it false, perverse, and heretical. He talked very reasonably, did his Reverence."

"So he wasn't conscious of any supernatural manifestations down there?"

"He underwent them all: illuminations, miraculous powers, ecstasy, everything. He doesn't deny, either, that these things happen there."

"Well, then, tell me, how does he explain it?"

"He simply doesn't. He said that the Church does not explain, but merely prescribes or prohibits. In short, he definitely refused to compromise the Church with any new and untried God. At least, that's what I understood him to mean. Do you know that I've bought that church up on the White Mountain?"

"Why?"

"It's the nearest one to Břevnov. It cost me three hundred thousand, man. Both in writing and by word of mouth I offered it to the Absolute down in the cellar to induce it to move over there. It's quite a pretty baroque church; and besides, I expressed my readiness to undertake any necessary alterations. And here's a queer thing: just a few steps from the church, at No. 457, there was a fine case of ecstasy the night before last—one of our erectors; but in the church itself nothing miraculous happened, nothing whatever. There was even one case right out in Vokovice and two in Košiře, while at the Petřin wireless station there's practically an epidemic of religion. All the wrieless operators on duty up there are sending out ecstatic messages of their own accord, a sort of new gospel to the world at large: God coming down again to the earth to ransom it, and so forth. Just imagine the scandal! Now the progressive papers are going for the Post Office, and the fur's fairly flying. They're screaming about Clericalism showing its horns, and rubbish of that kind. Nobody as yet suspects that this has any connection with the Karburator. Marek," Bondy added in a whisper, "I'll tell you something, but it's a dead secret. A week ago it attacked our Minister for War."

"Whom!" cried Marek.

"Hush, quietly. The Minister for War. He 'saw the light' all of a sudden in his villa at Dejvice. The following morning he assembled the garrison of Prague, talked to them about eternal peace, and exhorted the troops to become martyrs. Of course he had to resign at once. The papers stated that his health had suddenly broken down. And that's how matters stand, my friend."

"In Dejvice already!" groaned the engineer. "It's terrible, Bondy, the way it's spreading."

"It's amazing," said Bondy. "The other day a

man shifted his piano from the infected Mixa Street area out to Pankrác. In twenty-four hours the whole house was down with it."

Here the Chairman was interrupted. A servant entered to announce a caller in the person of Bishop Linda. Marek hurriedly rose to take his leave, but Bondy forced him to resume his seat, saying, "Just sit still and say nothing. The Bishop's really a charming man." At that moment the Suffragan Bishop Linda came into the room.

He was a small, jolly person with gold spectacles and a comical mouth puckered up in clerical fashion in pleasant childish folds. Bondy introduced Marek to him as the owner of the ill-omened cellar at Břevnov. The Bishop rubbed his hands with delight while the wrathful engineer spluttered out something about being "delighted to have the honour," with a dogged expression that said clearly, "Confound you for a canting humbug!" The Bishop pursed his lips and turned quickly to Bondy.

He began briskly, without beating about the bush. "I've come to you on a very delicate errand. Very delicate indeed," he repeated with relish. "We have been discussing your . . . ahem . . . your affair in the Consistory. His Eminence, the Archbishop, wishes to settle this regrettable incident with as little publicity as possible. You understand. This objectionable business about the miracles. Oh, I'm

sorry. I have no wish to hurt the feelings of Mr.
. . . er . . . the proprietor . . ."

"Please go on,"* Marek conceded gruffly.

"Well, then, in a word, the whole scandal. His
Eminence declares that from the standpoint of both
reason and faith there can be nothing more offen-
sive than this godless and blasphemous perversion of
the laws of Nature. . . ."

"I beg your pardon!" Marek broke out disgustedly. "Would you mind leaving the laws of
Nature to us? After all, we don't interfere with
your dogmas!"

"You are mistaken," cried the Bishop gaily.
"Quite mistaken. Science without dogma is only a
heap of doubts. What is worse, your Absolute
opposes the laws of the Church. It contradicts the
doctrine of the holy sacraments. It does not regard
the traditions of the Church. It seriously violates
the doctrine of the Trinity. It pays no attention to
the apostolic succession. It does not even submit to
the rites of exorcism. And so on. In short, it
behaves itself in a manner which we must severely
discountenance."

"Come, come," suggested Bondy propitiatingly.
"Up to the present its behaviour has been very . . .
dignified."

The Bishop raised his finger warningly.

"Up to the present; but we don't know how it will behave next. Look here, Mr. Bondy," he suddenly said in a confidential tone, "it is to your interest that there should be no unpleasantness. To our interest, too. You would like to settle it quickly, like a practical business man. So should we, as the representatives and servants of the Lord. We cannot permit the rise of some new God or possibly a new religion."

"Thank Heaven," Mr. Bondy sighed with relief. "I knew we should come to an agreement."

"Splendid!" cried the Bishop, his eyes sparkling with happiness through his spectacles. "An agreement, that's the thing. The venerable Consistory decided that in the interests of the Church it would place your . . . er . . . Absolute provisionally under its patronage. It would attempt to bring it into harmony with Catholic doctrine. It would proclaim the premises in Břevnov known as No. 1651 a miraculous shrine and place of pilgrimage. . . ."

"Oho!" growled Marek, and leaped to his feet.

"Permit me," said the Bishop with an imperious motion. "A miraculous shrine and place of pilgrimage—with certain conditions, of course. The first condition is that on the aforesaid premises the production of the Absolute should be limited to the smallest possible quantity, and that it should be only weak, almost innocuous, very much diluted Absolute, whose manifestations would be less uncontrollable and more irregular, rather as at Lourdes. Otherwise we cannot assume the responsibility."

"Very well," agreed Mr. Bondy. "And what else?"

"Further," continued the Bishop, "it is to be manufactured only from coal obtained at Male Svantovice. As you know, there is a miraculous shrine of the Virgin in that district, so that with the aid of this particular coal we might establish at No. 1651 Břevnov a centre for the worship of Our Lady."

"Undoubtedly," assented Mr. Bondy. "Anything more?"

"In the third place, you must bind yourself not to manufacture the Absolute at any other place or time."

"What?" cried G. H. Bondy, "and our Karburators——"

"—Will never come into operation, with the exception of the one at Břevnov, which remains the property of the Holy Church, and will be under her management."

"Nonsense," protested G. H. Bondy. "The Karburators *shall* be manufactured. In three weeks' time ten of them will be erected. In the first six months there will be twelve hundred. In the course of a year, ten thousand. Our arrangements have gone as far as that already."

"And I tell you," said the Bishop quietly and sweetly, "that at the end of that year not a single Karburator will be running."

"Why not?"

"Because mankind, whether believers or unbelievers, cannot do with a real and active God. We simply cannot, gentlemen. It is out of the question."

"And I tell you," Marek interposed vehemently, "that the Karburator *shall* be made. I'm in favour of them myself now. I mean to have them precisely because you don't want them. In spite of you, my Lord Bishop, in spite of all superstition, in spite of all Rome! And I mean to be the first to cry"—here the engineer took breath, then burst out with unmelodious enthusiam—"Success to the Perfect Karburator!"

"We shall see," said the Bishop with a sigh. "You gentlemen will live to be convinced that the venerable Consistory was right. In a year's time you will stop the manufacture of the Absolute of your own accord. But, oh, the damage, the devastation it will bring to pass in the meantime! Gentlemen, in the name of Heaven, do not imagine that the Church brings God into the world. The Church merely confines Him and controls Him. And you two unbelievers are loosing Him upon the earth like a

flood. The ship of Peter will survive even this
deluge; like the Ark of Noah, it will ride out this
inundation of the Absolute—but your modern
society," cried the Bishop with a mighty voice, *"that
will pay the price!"*

CHAPTER VI

"GENTLEMEN"—it was G. H. Bondy addressing the meeting of the Board of Directors of the M.E.C. (the Metallo-Electrical Company) held on February 20th—"I have to inform you that one building of our new group of factories at Vysočany has been completed and began production yesterday. In a very few days the standardized production of Karburators will be in full swing, beginning with eighteen finished machines per day. In April we expect to turn out sixty-five per day; by the end of July two hundred per day. We have laid down fifteen kilometres of private line, chiefly for our coal supply. Twelve boiler furnaces are now being erected. We have begun the building of new quarters for our workmen."

"Twelve boiler furnaces?" Dr. Hubka, the leader of the opposition, asked at a venture.

"Yes, twelve for the time being," confirmed Bondy.

"That's strange," Dr. Hubka declared.

"I ask you, gentlemen," said Bondy, "what is

45

there strange about having twelve boilers? For a huge group of factories like this . . ."

"Of course, of course," came from several quarters.

Dr. Hubka smiled ironically.

"And why the fifteen kilometres of railway line?"

"For the transport of coal and raw materials. We are reckoning on a daily consumption of eight truckloads of coal until we have things properly under way. I don't know what Dr. Hubka's objection to our getting coal in can be."

"I'll give you my objection," cried Dr. Hubka, leaping up. "It's that the whole business looks highly suspicious. Yes, gentlemen, extremely suspicious. Mr. Bondy has forced us to erect a factory for Karburators. The Karburator, he assured us, is the only power-supply of the future. The Karburator, as he expressly stated, can develop a thousand horse-power from a single bucket of coal. And now he is talking about twelve boiler furnaces and whole truckloads of coal for them. Gentlemen, I ask you, why then shouldn't a single bucket of coal give sufficient power for our whole factory? Why are we erecting boiler furnaces when we've got atomic motors? Gentlemen, if the Karburator is not an utter swindle, I don't see why our Chairman did not arrange for our own new factory to be equipped to be run by Karburator power. I don't see it, and no one else will see it. Why hasn't our Chairman sufficient confidence in these Karburators of his to install them in our establishment? Gentlemen, it's shockingly bad advertisement for our Karburators if their manufacturer himself will not or cannot use them. I beg you, gentlemen, to ask Mr. Bondy to give us his reasons. For my part, I have formed my own opinion. That is all I have to say, gentlemen."

Thereupon Dr. Hubka sat down resolutely, and victoriously blew his nose.

The members of the Board of Directors remained silent and dejected. Dr. Hubka's indictment was all too clear. Bondy did not raise his eyes from his papers; not a muscle of his face moved.

"M—m no," growled old Rosenthal, anxious for peace. "Our Chairman will explain. Yes, yes, it can all be explained, gentlemen, I think, m—m—er, yes—very satisfactorily. Dr. Hubka is surely mm—hm—hm—yes, yes—with regard to what he has told us."

The Chairman at last raised his eyes. "Gentlemen," he said quietly, "I have read you the expert report of our engineers on the Karburator. The facts are precisely as there stated. The Karburator is no swindle. We have already built ten of them for testing purposes. They all work perfectly. Here are the proofs. Karburator No. 1 drives the suction pump on the Sazava River, and has been running without attention for fourteen days. No. 2, the dredge on the Upper Vltava, is working spendidly. No. 3 is in the testing laboratory of the Brno Technical Institute. No. 4 was damaged in transport. No. 5 is supplying the city of Hradec Králové with light. That is the ten-kilo pattern. The five-kilo pattern, No. 6, is running a mill at Slany. No. 7 has been installed to provide central heating for a block of buildings in the New Town. Mr. Machat, the proprietor of that block, is with us to-day. Would you mind, Mr. Machat?"

The elderly gentleman of that name awoke as from a dream. "I beg your pardon?"

"We were asking how your new central-heating system is working."

"What? What heating do you mean?"

"In your new block of buildings," said Bondy gently.

"What block of buildings?"

"In your new houses."

"In my houses? I haven't any houses."

"Come, come, come!" Mr. Rosenthal exclaimed. "You put them up only last year."

"I did?" said Machat in tones of surprise. "Oh, yes, you're right, so I did. But, you see, I have given those houses away, now. I gave them all away."

Bondy looked at him very attentively. "And to whom did you give them, Mr. Machat?"

Machat flushed slightly. "Well, to poor people. I've let poor families occupy them. You see, I . . . I came to the conclusion that . . . well, in short, poor people have got them now, I mean."

Mr. Bondy kept his eyes on Machat like an examining magistrate. "Why, Mr. Machat?"

"I . . . I couldn't help it," Machat stammered. "It took me like that. Our lives should be holy, I mean."

The Chairman drummed nervously on the table. "And what about your family?"

Machat began to smile beatifically. "Oh, we're all of the same mind in that matter. Those poor people are such saints. Some of them are ill. My daughter is looking after them, you know. We've all changed so tremendously."

G. H. Bondy dropped his eyes. Machat's daughter Ellen, the fair-haired Ellen, with her seventy millions, tending the sick! Ellen, who was ready to be, who ought to be, who had half consented to be, Mrs. Bondy! Bondy bit his lip; things *had* turned out nicely!

"Mr. Machat," he began, in subdued tones, "I only wanted to know how the new Karburator was doing the heating on your premises."

"Oh, splendidly! It's so beautifully warm in every one of the houses! Just as though they were being warmed with eternal love! Do you know," said Machat rapturously, wiping his eyes, "whoever enters there becomes at one stroke a changed man. It is like Paradise there. We are all living as if we were in Heaven. Oh, come and join us!"

"You see, gentlemen," said Bondy, controlling himself with an effort, "that the Karburators work exactly as I promised you they would. I ask you to waive any further questions."

"We only want to know," cried Dr. Hubka pugnaciously, "why, in that case, you don't arrange for our new works to be run by Karburator power? Why should we use expensive coal for heating when we're supplying atomic energy to other people? Is Mr. Bondy disposed to let us have his reasons?"

"By no means," Bondy declared. "Our heating will be done with coal. For reasons known to myself, the Karburator system will not suit our purposes. Let that suffice, gentlemen. I regard the whole affair as a question of confidence in me."

Machat made himself heard. "If you only knew how wonderful it feels to be in a state of holiness! Gentlemen, take my sincere advice. Give away all that you possess! Become poor and holy! Deliver yourselves from Mammon, and glorify the one God!"

"Come, come," Mr. Rosenthal tried to calm him down. "We know you for a kind and upright man, Mr. Machat—yes, yes, extremely so. And I have every confidence in you, Mr. Bondy, you know. I tell you what, send me one of those Karburators for my own heating apparatus! I'll give it a trial, gentlemen. What's the use of all this talking? What about it, Mr. Bondy?"

"We are all brothers in God's sight!" continued the radiant Machat. "Gentlemen, let us give the factory to the poor! I move that we change the M.E.C. into a religious community of 'The Humble of Heart.' Let us be the seed from which the tree of God shall spring. The Kingdom of God on earth!"

"I demand a hearing," shouted Dr. Hubka.

"Come, now, Mr. Bondy," pleaded old Rosenthal in mollifying tones. "You see I am on your side! Lend me one of those Karburators, Mr. Bondy!"

"For God Himself is descending upon the earth," Machat continued in great excitement. "Hearken to His message: Be ye holy and simple; open your hearts to the infinite; let your love be unbounded. Let me tell you, gentlemen——"

"I demand the floor," yelled Dr. Hubka hoarsely.

"Silence!" shouted Bondy, pale and with gleaming eyes, as he rose with the whole authority of his massive frame. "Gentlemen, if the factory for Karburators does not suit your fancy, I will take it over under my own personal charge. I will compensate you to the last penny for all the expenditure so far incurred. I resign my position, gentlemen. I beg to take my leave."

Dr. Hubka darted forward. "But, gentlemen, I protest! We all protest! We will not part with the manufacture of Karburators! A spendid line like that, gentlemen! No, thank you, we are not to be hoodwinked into handing over a valuable business. With your permission, gentlemen———"

Bondy rang the bell. "Friends," he said gloomily, "we will leave this for the time being. It seems to me that our friend Machat is . . . er . . . slightly indisposed. As far as the Karburator is concerned, gentlemen, I guarantee you a dividend of one hundred and fifty per cent. I move that the discussion be now closed."

Dr. Hubka took the floor. "I move, gentlemen, that every member of the Board of Directors shall receive one Karburator for testing purposes, so to speak."

Bondy looked at all present. His features twitched. He tried to say something, but he only shrugged his shoulders and hissed between his teeth, "As you please."

CHAPTER VII

DEVELOPMENTS

"How do we stand in London?"

"M.E.C. shares were quoted at 1470 yesterday. The day before yesterday they were 750."

"Good!"

"Mr. Marek has been made an honorary member of ten learned societies, and is certain to be awarded the Nobel Prize."

"Good!"

"There's a rush of orders from Germany. Over five thousand Karburators wanted."

"Aha!"

"Nine hundred orders from Japan, too."

"Look at that now!'

"Czechoslovakia doesn't show much interest. Three fresh inquiries."

"Hm. That's all one might expect. A wretched state of affairs here, you know."

"The Russian Government wants two hundred immediately."

"Good! What's the total?"

"Thirteen thousand orders."

"Good! How far have we got with the buildings?"

"The division for atomic motor-cars has got the roof on. The section for atomic flying-machines will begin work during the week. We are laying the foundations for the atomic locomotive works. One wing of the department for ships' engines is already in operation."

"Wait a minute. You should start calling them automobiles, atomotors and atomotives, you know. How is Krolmus getting along with the atomic cannon?"

"He's already constructing a model at Pilsen. Our atomic cyclecar is doing its thirty thousandth kilometre on the Brussels racing-track. It has done two hundred and seventy kilometres an hour. We have had seventeen thousand orders for our half-kilo atomotors in the last two days."

"A minute ago you told me that the total was thirteen thousand."

"Thirteen thousand stationary atomic boilers. Eight thousand of the central-heating apparatus. Nearly ten thousand atomobiles. Sixty hundred and twenty atoplanes. Our A.7 has flown from Prague to Melbourne, Australia, without a stop; all on board safe and sound. Here is the telegram."

Bondy drew himself up. "Why, my young friend, that's splendid!"

"The agricultural machinery department has five thousand orders in. In the section for small power-engines, twenty-two thousand. One hundred and fifty atomic pumps. Three atomic presses. Twelve atomic blast furnaces. Seventy-five atomic wireless stations. One hundred and ten atomic locomotives, all for Russia. We have established general agencies in forty-eight different capitals. The American Steel Trust, the Berlin General Electric Company, the Italian Fiat, Mannesmann, Creusot, and the Swedish steel-works are all making us offers of amalgamation. Krupp's are paying any price for our shares."

"What about the new issue?"

"Thirty-five times over-subscribed. The financial papers predict a super-dividend of two hundred per cent. The other papers are talking of nothing but this business; politics, sport, technology, science, everything's Karburator. We've had seven tons of newspaper cuttings from our agent in Germany, four hundredweight from France, and a truckload from England. The scientific and technical literature dealing with atomotors, to be published this year, is estimated at sixty tons. The Anglo-Japanese war has been broken off owing to the lack of public interest. In England alone there are nine hundred thousand coal-miners out of work. There has been a rising in the Belgian coalfields; about four thousand killed. More than half the mines in the world have ceased working. The surplus petroleum in

Pennsylvania has set the oil-fields ablaze. The fire's still raging."

"The fire's still raging," repeated Bondy, as though in a dream. "The fire's still raging. My God, then, we have won!"

"The Chairman of the Mining and Smelting Company has shot himself. The Stock Exchange has simply gone mad. We stand at 8,000 to-day in Berlin. The Cabinet is in permanent sitting, and want to proclaim a state of siege. This isn't an invention, Chief, it's a revolution!"

The Chairman and the General Manager of the M.E.C. looked at each other in silence. Neither of them was a poet, but in that moment their very souls were singing.

The manager drew his chair closer and said in a low voice, "Chief, Rosenthal has gone crazy."

"Rosenthal!" exclaimed G. H. Bondy.

The manager nodded mournfully. "He has become an orthodox Jew, and he's gone in for Talmudic mysticism and Cabalism. He has given ten millions to the cause of Zionism. Not long ago he had a terrible quarrel with Dr. Hubka. You've surely heard that Hubka has joined the Bohemian Brethren."

"What, has Hubka got it too?"

"Yes, I think the Board of Directors must have caught it from Machat. You were not present at the last meeting, Chief. It was terrible; they talked religion until morning. Hubka moved that we hand over our establishments to the workers. Luckily, they forgot to take a vote on it. They were like men possessed."

Bondy gnawed at his fingers. "What on earth am I to do with them?"

"Hm, nothing whatever. It's a nervous disease of the age. Something of the sort crops up now and again in the papers, too, but they're so full of the Karburators that they haven't space for anything else. There's an appalling number of cases of religious mania. It's a physicial epidemic or something. The other day I saw Dr. Hubka preaching to a crowd of people in front of the Industrial Bank about seeking the inward light and making straight the path for God. Fearfully incoherent stuff. He wound up by performing miracles. Forst is at it too. Rosenthal is nothing short of insane. Miller, Homola and Kolator came out with a proposal for voluntary poverty. We can't possibly have another board-meeting. It's a regular madhouse, Chief. You'll have to take the whole idiotic business in hand."

"But, man, this is simply awful," groaned G. H. Bondy.

"It is indeed. Did you hear about the Sugar Bank? All the officials there were seized with it at one fell swoop. They opened the safes and gave away the money to anyone who came. They finished by burning bundles of banknotes on a bonfire in the main hall. Religious Bolshevism, I should call it."

"In the Sugar Bank? . . . Hasn't the Sugar Bank one of our Karburators?"

"Yes. For central heating. The Sugar Bank was the first to install one. Now the police have closed the Bank. Even the confidential clerks and the directors were affected."

"Send word round that the sale of Karburators to banks is forbidden."

"But why?"

"I forbid it, and that's enough! Let them do their heating with coal!"

"It's a bit too late. All the banks are already putting in our heating system. It's being installed in the Houses of Parliament and in all the Government departments. The central Karburator at Stvanice, which is to light the whole of Prague, is finished. It is a fifty-kilo monster, a magnificent machine. It is to be ceremoniously set in motion at six o'clock the day after to-morrow, in the presence of the President, the Burgomaster, the City Council, and the representatives of the M. E. C. You must be present. You of all people!"

"God forbid!" Mr. Bondy shouted, horror-stricken. "No, no, Heaven defend me from that! I will not go!"

"But, Chief, you must. We can't send Rosenthal or Hubka there. Why, they're raving mad. They would make dreadful speeches. It's the honour of the firm that's at stake. The Burgomaster of Prague has prepared a speech in our honour. The representatives of foreign Governments and the foreign Press will be there. It's to be a great occasion. As soon as the street lamps light up, military bands are going to play salutes and fanfares in the streets, the Male Voice Choirs and the other Choral Societies will sing, there'll be fireworks and a salute of a hundred and one guns, the Castle will be illuminated, and I don't know what. Chief, you simply must be there."

G. H. Bondy arose in great torment of spirit. "God! oh God!" he whispered, "if it be possible, remove this cup. . . ."

"Will you be there?" repeated the manager inexorably.

"God! oh God! why hast Thou forsaken me?"

CHAPTER VIII

THE DREDGE

THE dredge M. E. 28 stood motionless in the evening twilight above Stechovice. The Paternoster shovel had long since ceased heaving up the cold sand from the bed of the Vltava River. The evening was mild and calm, fragrant with new-mown hay and the breath of the woodlands. A tender orange glow still lingered in the north-west. Here and there a wave glittered with unearthly splendour amid the reflections of the sky—gleamed, murmured and blent itself with the shining surface of the stream. A skiff was coming towards the dredge from Stechovice. It made slow progress against the rapid current, and stood out upon the glowing river like a black water-beetle.

"Someone is coming over to see us," Kuzenda, the skipper, said quietly, from his seat in the rear of the dredge.

"Two of 'em," said Brych, the stoker, after a pause.

"Yes, and I know who it is, too," said Kuzenda.

"The sweethearts from Stechovice," said Brych.

"I'd better make them some coffee," Kuzenda decided, and went below.

"Now then, youngsters," Brych shouted to the boat. "To the left! Left! Give us your hand, lass. There we are. Up she comes!"

"Me and Joe," the girl announced on reaching the deck, "we—we'd like to——"

"Good evening," said the young workman who climbed up after her. "Where is Mr. Kuzenda?"

"Mr. Kuzenda is making coffee," said the stoker. "Take a seat. Look, there's someone else coming across. Is that you, baker?"

"That's me," a voice rang back. "Good evening, Mr. Brych. I've got the postman and the gamekeeper with me."

"Come up then, brothers," said Mr. Brych. "We can begin while Mr. Kuzenda is getting the coffee ready. Who else is coming?"

"I am," came a voice from the side of the dredge. "My name's Hudec, and I'd very much like to hear you."

"You are very welcome, Mr. Hudec," the stoker shouted down. "Come up, will you?—there's a ladder here. Half a minute and I'll give you a hand, Mr. Hudec, seeing you've never been here before."

"Mr. Brych," three people shouted from the bank.

"Send the boat across for us, will you? We'd like to come over."

"Go and fetch them over, you below," said Mr. Brych, "that all may hear the word of God. Brothers and sister, please sit down. It's not dirty here now that we do our heating with a Karburator. Brother Kuzenda will bring you some coffee, and then we can start. Welcome, young people. Come right up." With this Mr. Brych took his place by the opening down which ran the ladder to the interior of the dredge. "Halloa there, Kuzenda, ten on deck."

"Right!" cried a beard-muffled voice from the depths. "I'm just bringing it."

"Come, friends, sit down," said Brych, briskly indicating suitable seats. "Mr. Hudec, we have nothing but coffee here; I don't expect you'll mind."

"Why should I?" returned Mr. Hudec. "I just wanted to see your—to be present at your—séance."

"Our service," Brych mildly corrected him. "We are all brothers, here, you know. Let me tell you, Mr. Hudec, that I was a drunkard and Kuzenda was in politics, and the grace of God came upon us, and our brethren and sisters here," he said pointing round him, "come to us in the evenings to pray for the same gift of the spirit. The baker here had asthma, and Kuzenda cured him. Come now, baker, tell us yourself how it happened."

"Kuzenda laid hands on me," said the baker softly and rapturously, "and all at once such a feeling of warmth began to pour through my chest. You know, something just snapped in me, and I began to breathe as if I was flying about in the sky."

"Wait a bit, baker," Brych corrected him. "Kuzenda didn't lay his hands on you. He hadn't any notion he was going to work a miracle. He simply went like this with his hand, and then you said that you could breathe easily. That's the way it was."

"We were there when it happened," said the young girl from Stechovice. "And the baker had a ring of light around his head, and then Mr. Kuzenda charmed away my consumption, didn't he, Joe?"

The young fellow from Stechovic said, "That's the honest truth, Mr. Hudec. But what happened to me is queerer still. I wasn't straight, Mr. Hudec; I'd already been in jail for theft, and for another job besides. Mr. Brych here could tell you."

"Oh, it wasn't as bad as all that." Mr. Brych dismissed it with a wave of his hand. "All that you needed was grace. But there's some very queer things happen here, Mr. Hudec, on this spot. But perhaps you will find it out for yourself. Brother Kuzenda can give it you properly because he used to go to meetings before. Look, here he comes."

Everyone turned towards the opening leading

from the deck to the engine-room. From the open·
ing there emerged a bearded face, wearing the
forced, embarrassed smile of one who is being shoved
from behind and is trying to pretend that nothing is
happening. Mr. Kuzenda was visible now from the
waist up, carrying in both hands a large tin tray on
which stood cups and tins of preserves; he smiled
uncertainly as he rose higher and higher. His feet
could soon be seen on a level with the deck, and
still Mr. Kuzenda and his cups went on rising in
the air. About eighteen inches above the opening he
stopped and began groping with his feet. There he
hung unsupported in the air, apparently doing his
utmost to get his feet to the ground.

Mr. Hudec was like a man in a dream. "What is
the matter, Mr. Kuzenda?" he exclaimed, almost in
terror.

"Nothing, nothing," Kuzenda replied evasively,
still trying to draw himself down from the air with
his feet; and Mr. Hudec was reminded of a picture
of the Ascension that in his childhood had hung
above his little cot, and how Our Lord and the
Apostles in precisely the same manner were hanging
in the air and paddling with their feet, but showing
less amazement on their faces.

Suddenly Mr. Kuzenda moved forward and
floated, floated over the deck through the evening
air as though a gentle breeze might carry him away;

now and again he raised his feet as if he wanted to step out firmly or something, and he was visibly concerned for his cups.

"I say, come and take this coffee," he said hastily. Brych, the stoker, held both hands up to him and took charge of the tray and the cups. Then Kuzenda let his feet hang down, crossed his arms on his breast, and hung there motionless, with his head a little on one side, and said, "Welcome, brothers. Don't be afraid because I'm flying. It is only a sign. Will you take the cup with the flowers on, young lady."

The stoker passed the cups and tins round. No one dared to speak. Those who had never been there before gazed in wonder on the levitation of Kuzenda. The guests of longer standing sipped their coffee slowly, and seemed, between the sips, to be praying.

"Have you finished?" asked Kuzenda after a while, opening wide his colourless, rapt eyes. "Then I'll begin." So saying, he cleared his throat, meditated for a while, and began: "In the name of the Father! Brethren and sisters, on this dredge, where signs of grace are shown to us, we are gathered together for worship. We need not send away the unbelievers and mockers as the spiritualists do. Mr. Hudec came as an unbeliever, and the gamekeeper has been looking forward to a little bit of fun. You are both welcome; but listen so that you may see that it is by grace I know you. You, gamekeeper, drink far too much; you drive the poor from the forest, and curse and swear even when there is no need. Do it no more. And you, Mr. Hudec, are a better-class thief. You know very well what I mean. And you're shockingly bad-tempered. Faith will reform and redeem you."

Utter stillness reigned on the deck. Mr. Hudec gazed steadfastly at the floor. The gamekeeper sobbed and sniffed, and fumbled with trembling hands for his pocket.

"I know what it is, gamekeeper," said Kuzenda gently from above. "You'd like to smoke. Don't be afraid to light up. Make yourself quite at home."

"Look at the little fish," whispered the young girl, pointing down to the smooth surface of the Vltava. "Look, Joe, the carp have come to listen, too."

"They're not carp," came from the exalted Kuzenda. "They're perch or dace. And, Mr. Hudec, you mustn't worry about your sins. Look at me: I once cared for nothing but politics. And I tell you, that, too, is a sin. There's no need to weep, gamekeeper; I didn't mean to be hard on you. He who once experiences grace can see right into men's hearts. You can see into people's souls too, can't you, Brych?"

"I can," said Mr. Brych. "The postman here is thinking this minute how fine it would be if you could help his little daughter. She's got scrofula, hasn't she, postman? Mr. Kuzenda will help her right enough if you bring her here."

"It's easy to mock and talk about superstition," said Kuzenda. "Brothers, if anyone had told me about miracles and God before this, I should have laughed at him. That's the kind of man I was. When we got this new machine that runs without fuel for the dredge, all our dirty heavy work ceased. Yes, Mr. Hudec, that was the first miracle that happened here—this Karburator, that does everything by itself, as though it had a mind. Even the dredge floats by itself wherever it ought to go. And look how steady it is. Do you notice, Mr. Hudec, that the anchors aren't down? It stands still without being anchored, and floats off again when it's needed to clear the river-bed; it starts itself and stops itself. We, that's Brych and me, don't have to touch a single thing. Will anyone dare tell me that isn't a miracle? And when we saw all this, we began to think it over, didn't we, Brych, until it all became clear to us. This is a sacred dredge, it is an iron church, and we are only here as its priests. If in old times God could appear in a well or in an oak-tree, and sometimes even like a woman, as with the ancient Greeks, why should He not appear on a dredge? Why should He shun machinery? A machine is often cleaner than a nun, and Brych keeps everything here as bright and shining as if it was on a sideboard. However, that's by the way. And let me tell you, God is not so infinite as the Catholics assert. He is about six hundred metres in diameter, and even then is weak towards the edges. He is at His strongest on the dredge. Here He performs miracles, but on the bank He only does inspirations and conversions, and in Stechovice, with a favourable wind, you only notice a kind of holy fragrance. Not long ago some oarsmen from the Czech Rowing Club were paddling by in the *Lightning,* close to us, and grace descended on all of them. Such is His power. And what this God wishes us to do, one can only feel here within," Kuzenda declared, with an emphatic gesture towards his heart. "I know that He cannot bear politics and money, intellect, pride, and self-conceit. I know He dearly loves both men and beasts, that He is very glad when you come here, and that good deeds are pleasing to Him. He is a thorough democrat, brethren. We, Brych and me, that is, feel that every penny burns us until we've bought coffee for everybody. One Sunday recently, there were several hundred people here, even sitting on both banks of the river, and behold, our coffee multiplied itself so that there was enough for everybody . . . and what splendid coffee it

was! But such things, brethren, are only outward
appearances. The greatest miracle is the influence
He has on our feelings. It is so intensely beautiful
that it fairly makes one shiver. Sometimes you feel
as if you could die of love and happiness, as if you
were one with the water below, with all the animals,
with the very earth and stones, or as if gigantic
arms were holding you embraced; oh, words cannot
utter what you feel. Everything around you is
sounding and singing, you understand the speech of
voiceless things, the water and the wind, you see
deep into everything, how one thing is linked with
another and with you; at one stroke you grasp everything better than if you had read it in print. Sometimes it comes upon one like a fit, so that one foams
at the mouth; but often it acts quite slowly and
penetrates to one's tiniest little vein. And now,
brothers and sisters, do not be afraid; two police
officers are just coming across in a boat to 'disperse'
us because we are holding an unauthorized assembly.
Just keep calm and have faith in the God of the
dredge."

It was already dark; but the entire deck of the
dredge and the faces of those present were glowing
with a tender light. The splash of oars was heard
below the dredge, then the boat stopped alongside.
"Hi, there!" cried a man's voice. "Is Mr. Kuzenda
there?"

"Yes, he is here," answered Kuzenda in the voice of an angel. "Come right up, brethren of the police. I know that the innkeeper of Stechovice has laid information against me."

Two policemen mounted to the deck. "Which of you is Kuzenda?" asked the sergeant.

"I am, sir," said Kuzenda, rising higher in the air. "Kindly come up here to me, sergeant." And forthwith both police officers rose into the air and floated upwards towards Kuzenda. Their feet groped desperately for some support, their hands clutched wildly at the yielding air, and one could hear their quick and frightened breathing.

"Don't be afraid, officers," said Kuzenda beatifically, "and say after me this prayer: O God, our Father, who are incarnate in this vessel . . ."

"O God, our Father, who are incarnate in this vessel," repeated the sergeant in choking voice.

"O God, our Father, who are incarnate in this vessel," Mr. Hudec began in a loud voice, and he fell on his knees, and on the deck a chorus of voices mingled with his own.

CHAPTER IX

THE CEREMONY

CYRIL KEVAL, district reporter on the staff of
the Prague *People's Journal*, hurried into eve-
ning-dress for the occasion and dashed off to Stvanice
just after six o'clock in the evening, to write up the
ceremonial opening of the new Central Karburator
Electric Power Station for Greater Prague. He
shouldered his way through the curious crowds that
overflowed the whole Petrov quarter, penetrated
the three ranks of police, and reached a small concrete structure decorated with flags. From inside
the little building could be heard the objurgations of
the workmen, who were, of course, behind time with
the erecting of the machine, and were now trying to
catch up. The whole Central Power Station was
an insignificant affair, no bigger than a public con-
venience. Old Cvancara of the *Venkov* was walking
pensively up and down in front of it, looking somewhat like a meditative heron.

"Well, my friend," he said quietly to the young
journalist, "it's safe to bet on something happening
to-day. I've never yet seen a function where there

wasn't some silly incident or other. And I've been at it now, young fellow, for forty years."

"But it is amazing, isn't it, sir?" Keval returned. "Fancy this little building lighting the whole city of Prague and driving the trams and trains for sixty kilometres round, besides supplying power for thousands of factories and—and——"

Mr. Cvancara shook his head sceptically. "We'll see, my young friend, we'll see. Nothing nowadays can surprise any of us of the old guard, but"—and here Cvancara lowered his voice to a whisper—"well, just look round and you'll see that they haven't even got a reserve Karburator handy. Suppose this one broke down, or even, say, went up in the air, what then—do you see what I mean?"

Keval was annoyed at not having thought of this himself, so he dissented. "That's out of the question, sir," he began. "I have reliable information. This power station here is only for show. The real Central Station is somewhere else; it's . . . it's . . ." he whispered, and pointed with his finger, "right down underground, I mustn't say where. Haven't you noticed, sir, that they are continually repairing the streets in Prague?"

"They've been doing it these forty years," said Mr. Cvancara gloomily.

"Well, there you have it," Keval lied triumphantly. "Military reasons, you know. A huge system of underground passages, storehouses, powder-magazines, and so on. My information is quite trustworthy. They've got sixteen underground Karburator fortresses right round Prague. On the surface there's not a trace of it, only football fields, a mineral-water stand, or a patriotic monument. Ha, ha! Do you see now? That's why they're putting up all these memorials."

"Young man," observed Mr. Cvancara, "what does the present generation know of war? We could tell them something. Aha, here comes the Burgomaster."

"And the new Minister for War. You see, I told you so. The Director of the Technical Institute. The Chairman of the M.E.C. The Chief Rabbi."

"The French Ambassador, the Minister of Public Works. I say, my friend, we'd better see about getting inside. The Archbishop, the Italian Ambassador, the President of the Senate, the Chief of the Sokol organization; you'll find that there's somebody they've left out."

Just then Mr. Cyril Keval gave up his place to a lady, and so was separated from the doyen of the journalists and lost his place near the entrance through which the endless stream of the personages invited was pouring. Then the strains of the national anthem were heard, and the orders to the guard of honour rang out, proclaiming the arrival of the Chief of State. Accompanied by a retinue of gentlemen in top-hats and uniforms, the President advanced along the crimson carpet towards the little concrete structure. Mr. Keval stood on tiptoe, confounding himself and his politeness.

"I'll never get in now," he said to himself. "Cvancara is right," he went on ruminating. "They always do something silly. Fancy putting up that little hut for an imposing ceremony like this. Ah well, the Czechoslovak Press Bureau will supply the speeches, and one can soon work up the trimmings—deep impressiveness of the occasion, magnificent progress, enthusiastic reception for the President——"

A sudden hush within the building made itself felt outside, and someone began to reel off the official address. Mr. Keval yawned and sauntered round the little building with his hands in his pockets. It was getting dark. The guards were in full-dress uniform with white gloves and rubber truncheons. Crowds of people were standing tightly packed along the banks. The opening address was far too long, as usual. Who was it speaking, anyway?

Then Keval noticed a little window in the concrete wall of the Central Station about two metres from the ground. He looked around, then leapt up like a flash, caught hold of the grating, and drew his clever head up to the window. Aha, the speaker was the Burgomaster of Greater Prague, all red in the face;

beside him stood G. H. Bondy, Chairman of the
M.E.C., representing the contracting firm, biting his
lips. The President had his hand on the lever of the
machine, ready to press it down at a given signal:
an instant later the festal illuminations of the whole
of Prague would flare out, the bands would play,
the fireworks would begin to blaze.

The Minister of Public Works was turning and
twisting nervously; doubtless he was to speak when
the Burgomaster had finished. A young Army
officer was pulling at his tiny moustache, the
Ambassadors were pretending to be giving their
whole souls to the address, of which they understood
not a single word, two Trade Union delegates were
not moving an eyelash—in short, "the proceedings
passed off without a hitch," Mr. Keval said to himself as he jumped down again.

He then ran five times round the whole Stvanice
district, came back to the Central Power Station,
and again sprang up to the little window. The
Burgomaster was still speaking. Straining his ears,
Keval could hear ". . . And then came the disastrous period of the Battle of the White Mountain."
He dropped down the wall again quickly, sat down,
and lit a cigar. It was already very dark. Over-
head the little stars twinkled through the branches
of the trees. "It's surprising that they didn't wait
until the President pressed the lever to light up
too," Keval said to himself. Otherwise, Prague was

in darkness. The black stream of the Vltava rolled
on without a lamp reflected in its waters. Everything quivered with expectation of the solemn
moment that was to bring the light.

When Keval had finished his cigar, he went back
to the Power Station and once more hoisted himself
up to the little window. The Burgomaster was still
talking, and his face was now of a purple bordering
on blackness. The Chief of State was standing
with his hand on the lever, the personages present
were talking together in low tones, only the foreign
Ambassadors listened on unmoving. At the very
back, the head of Mr. Cvancara could be seen
nodding drowsily.

Sheer physical exhaustion brought the Burgomaster to an end, and the Minister of Public Works
began speaking. He was obviously cutting his
sentences down unmercifully to shorten his address.
The Chief of State was now holding the lever in his
left hand. Old Billington, the doyen of the Diplomatic Corps, had passed away on his feet, preserving
even in death the expression of an attentive listener.
Then the Minister put an end to his speech as
though with an axe.

G. H. Bondy raised his head, looked about with
heavy eyes, and said a few words, apparently something to the effect that the M.E.C. was handing over
its work to the public for the use and benefit of our
metropolis, and so concluded. The Chief of State

drew himself erect and pressed the lever. Then, in an instant, the whole of Prague shone out as a vast expanse of light, the crowds cheered, the bells in all the steeples began to swing, and from the Marianske fort there sounded the first boom of the cannon.

Still hanging to his grating, Keval looked around towards the city. Flaming rockets shot up from Střelecky Island; Hradčany, Petřin, and even Letna, were aglow with garlands of electric lamps, distant bands began competing with each other, illuminated biplanes circled above Stvanice, while the immense V 16 soared up from Vyšehrad all bedecked with lanterns. The crowds removed their hats, the police stood like statues, their hands raised to their helmets in salute. Two batteries boomed out from the bastions, answered by the monitors from near Karlín.

Keval again pressed his face to the bars to see the conclusion of the ceremonies over the Karburator taking place inside. The next instant he uttered a hoarse cry, rolled his eyes, and once more squeezed himself still closer to the window. Then he uttered something like "Oh, God!", loosened his hold on the grating, and dropped heavily to the earth. Before he had actually reached the ground, someone rushing away from the place knocked into him. Keval seized him by the coat, and the man looked round. It was G. H. Bondy; he was as pale as death.

"What has happened, sir?" Keval stammered. "What are they doing in there?"

"Let go of me," Bondy panted. "For Christ's sake, let go. And get out of here, as quick as you can."

"But what has happened to them in there?"

"Let me go," shouted Bondy; and knocking Keval back with his fist, he disappeared among the trees.

Trembling all over, Keval supported himself against the trunk of a tree. From the interior of the concrete building came sounds as of savages chanting a hymn.

A few days later the Czechoslovak Press Bureau published the following obscure statement:

Contrary to the reports issued by a local publication which have obtained some currency abroad, we are able to state on the very best authority that no improper incidents of any kind took place on the occasion of the formal opening of the Karburator Central Power Station. In connection with this, the Burgomaster of Greater Prague has resigned his office and has gone into the country to recuperate. Mr. Billington, doyen of the Diplomatic Corps, is, contrary to published reports, well and active. The fact is that all present declare that nothing in their experience has ever made so powerful an impression upon them. Every citizen has the right to fall to the earth and worship God, and the performance of miracles is not in conflict with any official position whatever in a democratic State. It is in any case decidedly improper to connect the Chief of State with regrettable incidents occasioned only by insufficient ventilation, combined with excessive strain upon the nerves.

CHAPTER X

SAINT ELLEN

A FEW days after these occurrences G. H. Bondy was wandering through the streets of Prague, a cigar between his teeth, thinking things over. Anyone who met him would have thought that he was looking at the pavement; but Mr. Bondy was really looking into the future. "Marek was right," he was saying to himself, "Bishop Linda even more so. It was simply impossible to bring God to earth without a confounded lot coming of it. People could do what they liked, but it was going to shake the banks and do goodness knows what with industry. A religious strike broke out at the Industrial Bank to-day. We installed a Karburator there, and within two days the officials declared the bank's property to be a sacred trust for the poor. That couldn't have happened when Preis was manager. No, it certainly would never have happened."

Bondy sucked at his cigar in great depression. "Well, what about it?" he said to himself. "Are we to throw the whole thing up? Orders worth twenty-three millions came in to-day. It can't be stopped now. It means the end of the world, or something.

In two years' time everything will have come down crash. There are several thousand Karburators at work in the world already, every one of them pouring forth the Absolute day and night. And this Absolute is fiendishly clever, too. It has an insane desire to exert itself, no matter how. There you are, it hasn't anything to do, for thousands of years it's had nothing to do, and now we've let it off the chain. Just look at what it's doing at the Industrial Bank, for instance. It keeps the bank's books all on its own, does the accounts, carries on the correspondence. It gives orders to the Board of Directors in writing. It sends its clients fervent epistles about showing love by works. What's the result? The Industrial Bank shares are mere waste paper: it would take a kilo of them to buy a bit of cheese. That's what happens when God starts meddling with banking.

"The Oberlander firm, a textile factory in Upice, is bombarding us with despairing telegrams. A month ago they put in a Karburator in place of a boiler. Splendid, the machines are going strong: all's well. But suddenly the spinning-jennies and looms begin to work all by themselves. When a thread breaks, it simply splices itself again, and on they go. The workmen just look on with their hands in their pockets. They're supposed to knock off at six o'clock. The spinners and weavers go home.

But the looms go running on by themselves. They
go on running all night and all day, for three whole
weeks, weaving, weaving, weaving without a pause.
The firm wires us: 'In the devil's name, take the
finished goods off us, send us raw material, stop the
machines!' And now it has got hold of the factory
of Buxbaum Brothers, Morawetz and Co., by sheer
long-range infection. There are no raw materials
in the place. They lose their heads and fling rags,
straw, earth, whatever comes handy, into the
machines; well, even that stuff, if you please, gets
woven into kilometres of towels, calico, cretonne,
and everything imaginable. There's a terrific up-
heaval; the prices of textiles are coming down with
a crash; England is raising her protective tariff; and
our neighbouring states are threatening us with a
boycott. And the factories are wailing, 'For the
love of Heaven, take the finished goods away at
least. Cart them away; send us men, lorries, motor
trains; stop the machines!' In the meantime, they're
suing us for damages. A damnable life! And we
hear the same thing from all sides, from everywhere
where a Karburator has been installed.

"The Absolute wants work. It clings furiously
to life. Once it created the earth! now it has flung
itself into manufacture. It has captured Liberec
and the Brno cotton works, Trutnov, twenty sugar
factories, sawmills, the City Brewery in Pilsen; it

is threatening the Skoda arsenal; it is busy at Jablonec and in the Jachymov mines. In many places people are dismissing their workmen; in others they've taken fright, closed the factories, and are just letting the machine go ahead inside. It's insane over-production. Factories that haven't got the Absolute are stopping production altogether. It's ruin.

"And I," said Mr. Bondy to himself, "am a patriot. I will not let our country be brought to ruin. Besides, there are our own establishments here. Very well, from to-day onward we will cancel all orders from Czechoslovakia. What has been done is done; but from this moment not a single Karburator shall be set up in the land of the Czechs. We'll flood the Germans and the French with them; then we'll bombard England with the Absolute. England is conservative, and won't have anything to do with our Karburators. Well, we'll drop them on her from airships like big bombs. We'll infect the whole industrial and financial world with God, and preserve only our own country as an island of civilization and honest labour free from God. It is a patriotic duty, so to speak, and besides, we have our own factories to consider."

The prospect gladdened G. H. Bondy's heart.

"At any rate we'll gain time to invent some sort of protective mask against the Absolute. Damn it,

I'll set aside three millions myself for purposes of research into protective measures against God. Better say two millions to start with. All the Czechs will go about wearing their masks, while all the rest —ha! ha!—will be getting drowned in the Absolute. At any rate their industries will go under."

Mr. Bondy began to look upon the world less darkly. "There's a young woman going by. Nice springy walk. I wonder what she looks like from the front." Mr. Bondy quickened his step, passed her, suddenly stepped respectfully to one side, then seemed to change his mind again, and turned on his heel so abruptly that he almost ran right into her.

"You, Ellen," he said hastily. "I had no idea, that—that——"

"I knew that you were following me," said the girl standing still with downcast eyes.

"You knew it?" said Bondy, greatly pleased. "I was just thinking about you."

"I could feel your bestial desires," said Ellen quietly.

"My what?"

"Your bestial desires. You did not recognize me. You only appraised me with your eyes as if I were for sale."

G. H. Bondy frowned. "Ellen, why do you wish to hurt my feelings?"

Ellen shook her head. "They all do it. They're

all alike, every one of them. One rarely meets a look that is pure."

Mr. Bondy pursed his lips for a whistle. Aha, so that's what it is! Old Machat's religious community!

"Yes," Ellen replied to his thoughts. "You ought to come and join us."

"Oh, of course," cried Mr. Bondy; and in his mind he said, "A nice girl like this! It's a shame."

"Why is it a shame?" asked Ellen gently.

"Oh, come, Ellen," protested Bondy. "You are a thought-reader. That isn't fair. If people were to read each other's thoughts they could never decently associate with one another. It's very indiscreet of you to know what I am thinking."

"What am I to do?" said Ellen. "Everyone who knows God has this same gift. Every one of your thoughts is born in my mind as soon as in yours. I don't read it, I have it myself. If you only knew how purifying it is when one can judge of every hidden baseness!"

"Hm," muttered Mr. Bondy, trembling lest anything should cross his mind.

"It is indeed," Ellen assured him. "It has cured me, with the help of God, of the love of riches. I should be ever so glad if the scales were to fall from your eyes, too."

"God forbid," exclaimed G. H. Bondy, horrified.

"But tell me, do you understand everything that you . . . er . . . see in people like this?"

"Yes, perfectly."

"Then listen to me, Ellen," said Bondy. "I can tell you everything, for you'd read it in me in any case. I could never marry a woman who would be able to read my thoughts. She could be religious to her heart's content, boundlessly charitable to the poor; I'm able to afford it, and besides, it's good publicity. I'd put up even with virtue, Ellen, for love of you. I'd put up with anything. I have loved you after my fashion, Ellen. I can tell you so because you can read it for yourself. But, Ellen, neither business nor society is possible without thoughts that are not disclosed. And marriage, above all things, is impossible without thoughts that are not disclosed. It is unthinkable, Ellen. And even if you find the holiest of men, don't marry him as long as you can read his thoughts. A little illusion is the only bond between mortals that never breaks. Saint Ellen, you must not marry."

"Why not?" said Saint Ellen in soft tones. "Our God is not opposed to nature; He only sanctifies it. He does not ask us to mortify ourselves. He bids us live and be fruitful. He wants us to . . ."

"Stop," Mr. Bondy interrupted her. "Your God doesn't understand. If He takes away our illusions He is doing something confoundly opposed to nature. He's simply impossible, Ellen, utterly impossible. If He were a reasonable being, He would realize it. He's either wholly inexperienced or else completely and criminally destructive. It's a great pity, Ellen. I haven't anything against religion, but this God doesn't know what He ought to want. Depart into the wilderness, Saint Ellen, with your second sight. You are out of place among us mortals. Farewell, Ellen; or rather—good-bye for ever."

CHAPTER XI

EXACTLY how it happened has not yet been established, but just at the very time when the little factory belonging to R. Marek, Engineer, 1651 Mixa Street, Břevnov, was garrisoned by detectives and surrounded by a cordon of police, unknown malefactors stole the original Marek Karburator. Despite the most active search, not a trace of the stolen machine was found.

Not long afterwards Jan Binder, the proprietor of a merry-go-round, was looking round the premises of a dealer in old iron in Hastal Square with a view to purchasing a little naphtha motor to run his roundabout and its orchestrion. The dealer offered him a big copper cylinder with a piston, and said it was a very economical motor; all one had to do was to shovel in a little coal, and it would run for months. Jan Binder was seized with a strange, almost blind faith in the copper cylinder, and he bought it for three hundred crowns. Then he hauled it away on a truck with his own hands to his merry-go-round, which was standing out of action near Zlichov.

Jan Binder took off his coat, unloaded the copper cylinder from the cart, and set to work whistling softly. He fixed a wheel on the axle where the fly-wheel used to be, and ran a belt over this wheel to another axle which drove the orchestrion with one end and the merry-go-round with the other. Then he oiled the bearings, put them into a wheel, and stood there, in his broad-striped jersey, with his hands in his pockets, puckering his lips for a whistle and waiting pensively to see what would happen next. The wheel went round three times, then stopped; presently it quivered, wobbled, and then began to turn quietly and smoothly. Then the orchestrion started with all its little drums and whistles, the merry-go-round gave itself a shake as if waking from sleep, creaked in all its joints, and began glidingly to revolve. The silver fringes gleamed, the white steeds with their showy trappings and red bridles seemed to set in motion their princely equipages, the deer with its wildly staring eyes swept round, poised as for a leap, the swans with their elegantly arching necks drew in a circle their white and sky-blue vessels; and so all a-glitter, and to the accompaniment of blaring music, the merry-go-round rotated its splendours before the unwinking eyes of the Three Graces painted on the orchestrion, now carried away on the rush of its own melodies.

Jan Binder still stood there with his lips pursed

and his hands in his pockets. He gazed upon his merry-go-round as though in a dream, seemingly entranced by something new and lovely. By this time he was no longer alone. A tear-stained dirty child dragged its young nurse up to the merry-go-round and stopped in front of it with great round eyes and mouth wide open, rigid with wonderment. The little nurse, too, opened wide her eyes and stood there like one enraptured. The merry-go-round performed its circuit with a strange resplendence, sublimity, stateliness, like a festal day . . . now whirling round with an impassioned velocity, now rocking gently like a vessel laden with the rich perfumes of India, now floating like a golden cloud high in the heavens; it seemed to soar upwards, sundered from the earth, it seemed to sing. But no, it was the orchestrion that was singing; now with the joyous voices of women mingling with a silvery rain of music falling from harps; and now it was the roar of a forest or a great organ, but from the depths of the forest birds fluted their songs and came and settled on your shoulders. Golden trumpets proclaimed the coming of a conqueror or, it might be, a whole army with flashing fiery swords. And who was it singing that glorious hymn? Thousands of people were waving branches of palm, the heavens opened, and, heralded by rolling drums, the song of God Himself descended upon the earth.

Jan Binder raised his hand, but at that moment
the merry-go-round stopped and leaned towards the
little child. The child tripped on to the merry-go-
round as if it were entering the open gates of Paradise, and the nursemaid followed as though in a
trance and seated it in one of the boats drawn by
swans. "Free rides to-day!" said Binder hoarsely;
the orchestrion burst out jubilantly, and the merry-
go-round began to turn as though it would soar up
into the sky. Jan Binder reeled. What could this
mean? Why, it wasn't the merry-go-round that was
turning now, but the whole earth was spinning round
and round. The Zlichovsky Church was describing
a gigantic curve, the Podol Sanatorium and Vyšehrad
were setting off together for the other bank of the
Vltava. Yes, the whole earth was turning about the
merry-go-round, circling faster and faster, humming
like a turbine; only the merry-go-round stood firm
in the centre, rocking gently like a ship with white
horses, deer and swans roving about the deck, and
a little child leading its nurse by the hand and strok-
ing the animals. Yes, yes, the earth was spinning
furiously, and only the merry-go-round was a lovely
island of quiet and repose. And Jan Binder, dizzy
and sick, raised his arms, and let the mad earth carry
him staggering towards the merry-go-round, seized
one of the rods, and swung himself up on to its
peaceful deck.

Now he could clearly see how the earth was heaving and tossing like a stormy sea. And look, there were terrified people rushing out of their houses, waving their hands, stumbling and falling as though borne along by a gigantic whirlwind. Holding tightly to his rod, Binder stooped down to them and shouted, "Here, people, this way!" And the people seeing the shining merry-go-round calmly uplifted above the reeling earth, staggered towards it. Gripping the rod, Binder held out his free hand and pulled them up from the heaving earth: children, grandmothers, old men, all stood on the deck of the merry-go-round, taking breath again after their terrible fright, and looking down in dismay upon the earth spinning below them. Binder had just helped them all up, when a little black puppy came running by, yelping with fear, and tried to leap aboard; but the earth carried him faster and faster round the merry-go-round. Binder squatted down, reached out his hand, and grabbed the puppy by the tail, and lifted it into safety.

Then the orchestrion played a song of thanksgiving. It sounded like a chorus of survivors of a shipwreck, with the rough voices of the sailors mingling with the prayers of children. Over the unleashed tempest there bent a rainbow of melody (in B minor) and the heavens opened in the happy radiance of pizzicati on the violins. The castaways on Binder's merry-go-round stood there silent with their heads bare. The women's lips moved softly in silent prayer, and the children, forgetting the horrors they had passed through, plucked up courage to stroke the hard muzzle of the deer and the supple neck of the swan. The white horses patiently allowed the little limbs to clamber into the saddles; sometimes one of them neighed or pawed knowingly with his hoof. The earth was turning more slowly now, and Jan Binder, a tall figure in his sleeveless striped jersey, began in his unpractised style to make a speech.

"Well, good people, here we have landed out of the whirl and confusion of the world. Here we have peace amid the storm. Here we are with God, as safe as in our beds. It is a sign that we should flee from the tumult of the world and find refuge in the arms of God. Amen." Thus and in like manner spoke Jan Binder, and the people on the merry-go-round listened as if they were in church.

At last the earth stopped spinning, the orchestrion played a soft and reverent voluntary, and the people jumped down from the merry-go-round. Jan Binder told them that there was no charge, and dismissed them, converted and uplifted. And when towards four o'clock the mothers and children and the old pensioners were taking their afternoon walk between Zlichov and Smichov, the orchestrion again began to

play, and the earth once more went flying round, and
again Jan Binder brought everybody safe on to the
deck of the merry-go-round and calmed them with
a suitable address. At six o'clock people came from
their day's work, sweethearts emerged at eight, and
at ten the pleasure-seekers left the public-houses and
picture-palaces; all of them in turn were overcome
by the dizzy whirling of the earth, brought to safety
in the embrace of the merry-go-round, and strength-
ened for their future life by the apt exhortations of
Jan Binder.

After a week of this hallowed work, Binder's
merry-go-round forsook Zlichov and went roaming
along the bank of the Vltava up to Chuchle and
Zbraslav, and so reached Stechovice. It had been
working in Stechovice for four days with tremendous
power, when an incident of a somewhat mysterious
character took place.

Jan Binder had just finished his sermon and dismissed his new disciples with a blessing. At that
moment there approached out of the darkness a
black and silent body of people. At their head
walked a tall, bearded man, who went straight up to
Binder.

"Now then," he said, trying to master his excitement, "pack up at once, or——"

Binder's adherents heard this and returned to
their teacher. Conscious of having his people at

the back of him, Binder declared firmly, "Not till it rains."

"Control yourself, sir," said another excited man. "It's Mr. Kuzenda speaking to you."

"Leave him to me, Mr. Hudec," cried the bearded man. "I'll soon settle with him myself. I'm telling you for the second time; clear out with that thing or, in the name of the Lord, I'll smash it up for you."

"And as for you," said Jan Binder, "get out of here or, in the name of the Lord, I'll knock the teeth out of your head."

"God Almighty!" shouted Brych, the stoker, forcing his way through the crowd to the front. "Just let him try!"

"Brother," said Kuzenda soothingly, "let us first try to settle it quietly. Binder, you are carrying on foul witchcraft here, and we'll not put up with it so close to the sacred shrine of our dredge."

"Your dredge is a fraud!" said Binder decisively.

"What did you say?" cried Kuzenda, cut to the quick.

"Your dredge is a fraud!"

What happened next it is hard to disentangle into any logical sequence. It seems that the first blow was struck by the baker from Kuzenda's camp, but Binder landed him a blow on the head with his fist. The gamekeeper struck Binder on the chest with his gunstock, but directly afterwards he lost his gun, and

some Stechovice youth from Binder's camp used it
to knock out Brych's front teeth and smash Mr.
Hudec's hat in. Kuzenda's postman tried to throttle
a youth on Binder's side. Binder leaped forward to
help the boy, but a girl from Stechovice flung herself
on him from behind, and bit him in the arm just
where he had had the Bohemian lion tattooed. One
of Binder's party drew a knife, and Kuzenda's
followers seemed to be falling back, but a smaller
group of them dashed on to the merry-go-round and
broke off the deer's antlers and the elegantly arching
neck of one of the swans. The merry-go-round gave
a deep groan and heeled over, its roof falling right
upon the struggling mob. Kuzenda was struck by
a pole and knocked unconscious. It all happened in
darkness and silence. When people came rushing
up, Binder had a broken collar-bone, Kuzenda lay
there unconscious, Brych was spitting out teeth and
blood, and the girl from Stechovice was sobbing
hysterically. The rest had fled.

CHAPTER XII

DOCTOR BLAHOUS

THAT youthful savant Doctor Blahous, Ph.D., only fifty-five years of age, and now Lecturer in Comparative Religion at the University of Prague, rubbed his hands as he sat down before his quarto sheets of paper. With a few swift strokes he set down his title—"Religious Phenomena of Recent Times"—and began his article with the words: "The controversy over the definition of the idea of 'religion' has lasted ever since the days of Cicero"; then he gave himself up to his thoughts.

"I'll send this article to the *Prague Times*," he said to himself, "and just you wait, my revered colleagues, and see what a stir it will make! It's lucky for me that this religious epidemic has broken out just now! It will make it a very topical little article. The papers will say, 'That youthful savant, Dr. Blahous, has just published a penetrating study,' etc. Then I'll be given the Assistant Professorship, and old Regner will burst with fury."

Whereupon the youthful savant rubbed his wrinkled hands until the bones cracked blithely, and again began to write. When towards evening his landlady came to inquire what he would like for supper, he was already on the sixtieth page, among the Fathers of the Church. At eleven o'clock (and page 115) he had arrived at his own definition of the idea of religion, which differed from his predecessor's by precisely one word. After this he dealt succinctly with the methods of the exact science of religion (with a few shrewd hits at his opponents), and so brought to an end the brief introduction to his little article.

Shortly after midnight our lecturer wrote the following passage: "It happens that quite recently various phenomena of a religious and occult character have occurred which deserve the attention of the exact science of religion. Although its main purpose is undoubtedly to study the religious customs of nations long since extinct, nevertheless even the living present can afford the *modern* [Dr. Blahous underlined the word] student numerous data which *mutatis mutandis* throw a certain light on cults long vanished, which can only be the subject of conjecture."

Then, with the aid of newspaper reports and evidence given verbally, he gave a description of Kuzendism, in which he found traces of fetish-worship and even totemism (the dredge being made a sort of Totem God of Stechovice). In the case of the Binderians, he worked out their relationship to the

Dancing Dervishes and ancient orgiastic cults. He touched upon the phenomena witnessed at the opening of the Power Station, and deftly showed their connection with the fire-worship of the Parsees. In Machat's religious community he discovered the characteristics of the fakirs and ascetics. He cited various examples of clairvoyance and miraculous healing, which he compared very aptly to the magic practised by the old negro tribes of Central Africa. He went on to deal with mental contagion and mass-suggestion, introducing historical references to the Flagellants, the Crusades, Millenarianism and "running amok" among the Malays. He threw light upon the recent religious movement from two psychological points of view, ascribing it to pathological cases in degenerate hysterical subjects, and to a collective psychical epidemic among the superstitious and mentally inferior masses. In both cases he demonstrated the atavistic occurrence of primitive forms of worship, the tendency to animistic pantheism and shamanism, a religious communism reminiscent of the Anabaptists, and a general surrender of reasoning power in favour of the grossest impulses of superstition, witchcraft, occultism, mysticism, and necromancy.

"It is not for us to decide," Dr. Blahous went on writing, "to what extent this is due to quackery and imposture on the part of individuals bent on exploiting human credulity; a scientific inquiry would doubtless show that the alleged 'miracles' of the thaumaturgists of to-day are only old and well-known devices of trickery and suggestion. In this connection we would recommend the new 'religious communities,' sects, and circles now daily springing into existence to the attention of our police authorities and psychoanalysts. The exact science of religion confines itself to establishing the fact that all these religious phenomena are at bottom nothing but examples of barbaric atavism, and a hotch-potch of the most rudimentary forms of worship still subconsciously active in the human imagination. It has only needed a few fanatics, charlatans, and notorious swindlers to revive among the peoples of Europe, under the veneer of civilization, these prehistoric elements of religious belief."

Dr. Blahous got up from his desk. He had just finished the three hundredth and forty-sixth page of his little article, but still he did not feel weary. "I must think out an effective finish," he said to himself; "some reflections on progress and science, on the suspicious benevolence of the Government towards religious heterodoxy, and on the necessity of presenting a fighting front to reaction, and so forth."

The youthful savant, borne on the wings of his enthusiasm, went to the window and leaned out into

the quiet night. It was half-past four in the morning.
Dr. Blahous looked out on the dark street, shivering
a little with the cold of the night. Everywhere was
the stillness of death, not a glimmer of light showed
in any human habitation. The Lecturer raised his
eyes to the sky. It was already paling a little, but
it still shone in its infinite sublimity, sown with stars.
"How long it is since I looked at the sky!" came
suddenly into the scholar's mind. "Good heavens, it
is more than thirty years!"

And then he felt a delicious coolness about his
brow, as though someone had taken his head in cool
and spotless hands. "I'm so lonely," the old man
sighed, "so terribly lonely all the time! Yes, stroke
my hair a little. Alas, it is thirty long years since
anyone's hand was laid upon my brow!"

Dr. Blahous stood there in the window, stiff and
shaking. "There is something here all about me,"
he suddenly perceived with a sweet and overwhelming emotion. "Dear God, I am not alone after all!
Someone's arm is around me, someone is beside me;
oh, if he would only stay!"

If his landlady had entered the room a little later,
she would have seen him standing in the window
with both arms raised on high, his head flung back,
and an expression of the utmost rapture on his face.
But then he shuddered, opened his eyes, and as if in
a dream went back to his desk.

"On the other hand, however, it is impossible to doubt," he wrote rapidly, heedless of all that he had already written, "that God cannot now reveal Himself otherwise than in primitive forms of worship. With the decay of faith in modern times our connection with the old religious life has been broken. To bring us back to Him, God must begin again from the beginning and do as He did with the savages in olden times: at first He is an idol, a fetish; the idol of a group, a clan or a tribe; He animates all nature and works through a witch-doctor. This evolution of religion is being repeated before our eyes, beginning with its prehistoric forms and working upwards to the loftier types. It is possible that the present religious wave will divide into several streams, each striving for supremacy to the disadvantage of the others. We must expect an era of religious struggles which will surpass the Crusades in their fury and obstinacy and the last World Wars in their scope. In our godless world the Kingdom of Heaven cannot be established without great sacrifices and confusion of doctrine. Nevertheless I say unto you: Give yourself up with your whole beings to the Absolute; believe in God, in whatsoever form He may declare Himself to you. Behold even now He cometh to set up on our earth, and perchance on other planets of our system also, the everlasting Empire of God, the Czardom of the Absolute. Ere it is too late, I say yet again unto you: Humble yourselves before Him!"

This article by Dr. Blahous did actually appear. Not in its entirety, to be sure. The editor published part of his discussion of the new sects and the whole of his conclusion, with a cautious note to the effect that this paper by the youthful savant was certainly characteristic of our times.

Blahous's article did not cause any stir, for it was overshadowed by other events. Only that youthful savant, Dr. Regner, Lecturer in Philosophy, read it with immense interest and afterwards proclaimed in various places: "Blahous is impossible. Utterly impossible. How on earth can a man have the nerve to pose as an expert on religion when he actually believes in God?"

CHAPTER XIII

THE CHRONICLER'S APOLOGY

AND now permit the chronicler of the Absolute to call your attention to his painful situation. First of all, he is in the act of writing Chapter XIII, well aware that this unlucky number will have a fatal influence on the clarity and completeness of his exposition. There is going to be a mix-up of some kind in this unfortunate chapter, you may be sure. Of course, the author could quite calmly head it Chapter XIV, but the observant reader would feel that he had been cheated out of Chapter XIII, and no one could blame him, since he has paid to have the whole narrative. Besides, if you are afraid of the number thirteen, you have only to skip this chapter. It will certainly not cause you to lose much light on the obscure affair of the Factory for the Absolute.

But the other embarrassments of the chronicler are much more serious. He has described as coherently as he could the origin of the factory and its prosperity. He has called your attention to the occurrences due to certain of the Karburator cylinders in Mr. Machat's buildings, at the Zivno

Industrial Bank, in the textile works at Upice, aboard Kuzenda's dredge, and on Binder's merry-go-round. He has described the tragic experience of Blahous, the result of long-range infection, induced by the free and mobile Absolute, which had evidently begun to spread in a serious fashion, although after no definite plan.

But now you must remember that since the beginning of the whole affair countless thousands of Karburators of the most diverse types had been manufactured. Trains, flying-machines, automobiles, and ships driven by this most economical of all motors discharged along their routes whole clouds of the Absolute, just as in other days they used to leave a trail of dust, smoke, and smells. You must remember that thousands of factories all over the world had already scrapped their old boilers and equipped themselves with Karburators; that hundreds of Government departments and offices, hundreds of banks, exchanges, wholesale and export firms, as well as huge restaurants, hotels, military barracks, schools, theatres, tenements, thousands of newspaper offices and clubs, cabarets, and households were being heated by the latest M.E.C. Central-Heating Karburator. You must remember that the Stinnes interests with all their ramifications had amalgamated with the M.E.C., and that the American Ford works had flung themselves into mass-production

which hurled thirty thousand finished Karburators
out upon the world every day.

Well, bearing all this in mind, just recall what
happened with each of those Karburators whose
history has been presented to you. Multiply these
incidents a hundred thousand times, and you will
grasp at once the unhappy position of the present
chronicler. How gladly he would journey with you
after each new Karburator, see it loaded on the
wagon, and offer a bit of hay or bread or a lump
of sugar to the heavy draught-horses, with their
broad and kingly backs, which drag the new copper
cylinders on the rattling lorry to the factory! How
gladly he would look on while they set it up, standing
with his hands behind his back and giving the
erectors his advice, and then wait until it was set in
motion! How eagerly then he would peer into
people's faces to note when "it" would begin to
affect them, when the Absolute would creep into their
being by the nose or ears or any other part, and
begin to dissolve the hardness of their nature, over-
power their personal tendencies, and cure their
moral wounds; to watch the Absolute turn them up
with its heavy plough, warm them, master them, and
shape them anew; to see it lay open to them a world
so marvellous and yet intrinsically so human, of
wonders, ecstasy, enlightenment, inspiration and
belief! For you must know that the chronicler

admits that he is incapable of writing a history. Where the historian uses the press or pounder of his historical learning, documentary lore, abstracts, synthesis, statistics, and other professional devices, to squeeze thousands and hundreds of thousands of little vital personal incidents into a dense and arbitrary conglomerate known as "a historical fact," "a social phenomenon," "a mass movement," "evolution," "the mind of the race," or "historical truth" in general, the chronicler sees only the individual cases and even finds them pleasing in themselves.

Now suppose that he had to describe and explain, say, pragmatically, progressively, theoretically, and synthetically, the "religious wave" which swept over the whole world before the year 1950. Once he sees this grandiose task before him, he begins collecting the "religious phenomena" of his own time; and there, in the course of these researches, he comes, for example, upon Jan Binder, ex-variety artiste, wandering from place to place in his striped jersey with his atomic merry-go-round. Historical synthesis, of course, requires the chronicler to omit the striped jersey, the merry-go-round, even Jan Binder himself, and retain as the "historical nucleus" or scientific result, only the discovery that "these religious phenomena from the very outset affected the most diverse classes of society."

Well, then, the chronicler must here and now con-
fess that he cannot cast aside Jan Binder, that he is
fascinated by his merry-go-round, and that even that
striped jersey of his interests him far more than
any "synthetic outline" whatever. To be sure, this
displays complete scientific incompetence, empty
dilettantism, the narrowest historical outlook, or
anything else you like; yet if the chronicler could give
rein to his personal inclinations, he would go off on
his travels with Jan Binder as far as Budejovice,
then to Klatovy, Pilsen, Zlutice, and so on. It is with
regret that he leaves him in Stechovice and waves
his hand and cries, "Good-bye, Binder, you sturdy
fellow, and good-bye, merry-go-round! We shall
never meet again."

Bless my soul, it was with just the same feeling
that I left Kuzenda and Brych on the Vltava dredge.
I should have liked to spend many and many an
evening with them, for I love the Vltava and all
running water in general, and evenings on the water
in particular, and I took an unusual liking to Mr.
Kuzenda and Mr. Brych as well. As for Mr. Hudec,
the baker, the postman, the gamekeeper, and the
sweethearts from Stechovice, I believe that they, too,
would be worth knowing intimately, as anyone is, as
all of you are, as is every living human being. But
I must push on, and I have hardly time enough to
wave my hat to you. Good-bye, Mr. Kuzenda;

good-night, Mr. Brych. My thanks for that one evening on board the dredge.

Of you, too, Dr. Blahous, I must take my leave. I should like to spend many a year with you and describe your whole career . . . for is not the life of a university lecturer rich and exciting, after its fashion? Give my regards to your landlady at least.

Everything there is, is worth observing.

And that is why I should like to accompany each new Karburator on its way. I should become acquainted with fresh people every day, and so would you, and that is always worth while. Just to peep through one's spyglass into their lives, to see their hearts, to watch their personal faith and personal salvation come into being, to linger amid the new marvels of human saintliness—that is what would lure me on! Just picture to yourself a beggar, a ruling chief, a bank-manager, an engine-driver, a waiter, a rabbi, a major, a writer on political economy, a cabaret comedian, men of every possible calling; and imagine a miser, a sensualist, a glutton, a sceptic, a hypocrite, a sneak, a career-hunter, men of every possible human passion—what diverse, endlessly varying, strange and surprising instances and phenomena of heavenly grace (or, if you like, poisoning with the Absolute) one could meet, and how absorbing it would be to study each one of them. What gradations of faith there would be, from the ordinary believer to the fanatic, from the penitent to the miracle-worker, from the convert to the fiery apostle. If one could only embrace it all! If one could only extend a hand to each of them! But it is useless; that great work will never be completed, and the chronicler, having renounced the honour of distilling scientifically all his historical material, turns away with sorrow from the individual cases which it is not permitted him to relate.

I wish I could stay a little longer with Saint Ellen! I wish I need not treacherously abandon our friend, R. Marek, undergoing a rest cure at Spindelmühl! I wish I could reveal the workings of the brain of that industrial strategist, G. H. Bondy. All in vain; the Absolute has already flooded the world, and has become a mass-phenomenon; and the chronicler, regretfully looking backward, must reconcile himself to a summary description of a few of the social and political events which inevitably ensued.

Come, then, let us enter upon a new range of facts.

CHAPTER XIV

THE LAND OF PLENTY

IT has often happened to the chronicler (and surely to many of his readers) that when for any reason whatever he has gazed at the night sky and the stars, and realized with mute amazement their prodigious number and their inconceivable distance and dimensions, and told himself that each of those glittering dots was a gigantic flaming world or a whole living planetary system, and that there were possibly billions, say, of such dots; or when he has looked down to a far horizon from a high mountain (it happened to me in the Tatras), and has seen beneath him fields and woods and mountains, and right in front of him dense forest and grass lands, all of it more than luxuriant, running riot, life exuberant and alarming in its richness—and when he has noted in the grass myriads of blossoms, tiny beetles, and butterflies, and has mentally multiplied this mad profusion by the vast expanses stretching away before him to Heaven knows where, and has added to these expanses the millions of other expanses equally crowded and luxuriant, which compose the surface of our earth; at such a moment it has often happened that the chronicler has bethought him of the Creator, and has said to himself: "If someone made or created all this, then we must admit that it is a terrible waste. If anyone wanted to show his power as a Creator, there was no need to create such an insane quantity of things. Excess is chaos, and chaos is something like insanity or drunkenness. Yes, the human intellect is staggered by the over-profusion of this creative achievement. There is simply *too much* of it. It's boundlessness gone mad. Of course, He who is Infinite from His very birth is accustomed to huge proportions in everything, and has no proper standard (for every standard implies finiteness) or, rather, has no standard whatsoever."

I beg you not to regard this as blasphemy; I am only endeavouring to set forth the disproportion between human ideas and this cosmic superabundance. This wanton, purposeless, well-nigh feverish excess of everything that exists appears to the sober human eye more like creativeness run wild than conscientious and methodical creation. That is what I wish to say, with all due respect, before we return to our story.

You are already aware that the process of perfect combustion invented by Marek practically proved the presence of the Absolute in every form of matter. One might put it this way (only as a hypothesis, of course), that before the creation of

all things the Absolute existed in the form of an
Infinite Free Energy. For some cogent physical or
moral reason, this Free Energy began to be creative.
It became Working Energy, and following the laws
of inversion, it was transformed into a state of
Infinite Imprisoned Energy. It lost itself somehow in its own handiwork, i.e. in created matter,
and remained there latent, as if under a spell.
And if this is hard to understand, I cannot help
you.

And now, apparently as a result of the perfect
combustion effected by Marek's atomic motors, this
imprisoned energy was liberated, freed of the fetters
of matter which had held it fast. It became once
more Free Energy or active Absolute, as free as it
was before the Creation. It was the sudden release
of that same inscrutable and unresting power which
had already manifested itself once in the Creation of
the World.

If the whole cosmos at once were to undergo
complete combustion, the first act of creation might
be repeated; for that would indeed be the end of
the world, a complete liquidation which would make
possible the establishment of a new world-firm,
Cosmos the Second. Meanwhile, as you know,
Marek's Karburators were only burning up the
material world by kilogrammes at a time. Being
thus released in small quantities only, the Absolute

either did not feel sufficiently strong to begin creating again at once, or perhaps did not wish to repeat itself. Anyhow, it decided to express itself in two ways, one of them to some extent traditional and the other distinctly modern.

The traditional manner in which it began to exert itself was, as you already know, the religious one. This embraced all varieties of illumination, conversion, moral effects, miracles, levitations, ecstasies, predictions, and, above all, religious faith. Here the Absolute burst into the personal and social life of the people over paths already well trodden, but to an extent hitherto unheard of. After a few months of its activity there was practically not a single person on earth who had not experienced, if only for a moment, that religious shock by which the Absolute made known its presence to his soul. We will return to the subject of this psychological onset of the Absolute later on, when it will be necessary to depict its catastrophic consequences.

The other form of manifestation of the existence of the Absolute at large was something entirely new. The Infinite Energy which had once busied itself with the creation of the world apparently took cognizance of the altered conditions, and flung itself into manufacture. It did not form something out of nothing, but it made finished goods out of raw material. Instead of indulging in pure creation, it took its place at the machines. It became the Infinite Artisan.

Suppose that some factory or other, say a place where tacks were manufactured, had installed a Perfect Karburator in place of a steam-engine as the cheapest form of plant. The Absolute constantly emanating from the atomic motor learnt the whole process of manufacture in a single day, by virtue of its innate intelligence, and flung itself with all its uncontrollable energy or, perhaps, ambition into this occupation. It began to manufacture tacks on its own account. Once it started, nothing could stop it. Without anyone in control of it, the machine vomited forth tacks. The supplies of iron ready to be manufactured into tacks raised themselves of their own accord, one piece after another, thrust themselves through the air, and inserted themselves in the proper machines. It was at first an uncanny thing to see. When these supplies were exhausted, iron sprouted out of the earth, the ground round the factory exuded pure iron as if it were being drawn by suction from the depths of the earth. This iron then raised itself into the air to the height of about one metre and slid jerkily into the machinery *as if it were being pushed in.* Please note this carefully; I may have said "the iron raised itself" or "the iron slid," but all eye-witnesses give it as their impression that the iron was *lifted* by sheer force by an inexorable but invisible power, and with a might so manifest and concentrated that they were seized with horror. It was plain to the eye that it was being done by the exercise of *terriffic effort*.

Probably some of you have toyed with spiritualism and have seen something of "table-lifting." If so, you will bear me out in this—that the table certainly did not rise as though it had lost its material weight, but rather moved with a sort of spasmodic effort; it creaked in all its joints, and quivered, and fairly reared, until finally it leaped up in the air as if lifted by a power which was struggling with it for mastery.

But how am I to describe the frightful, silent struggle which forced iron to raise itself from the depths of the earth, which pressed it into bars, threw these into the machines, and smashed them up into tacks? The bars twisted like withies, fought against the motion that pushed them forward, rattled and grated amid the silence of that which wrestled with them, soundless and substanceless. All contemporary reports speak of the horror of the scene. It was a very miracle, but do not imagine that a miracle is something fabulously easy and effortless; it rather seems that the performance of a genuine miracle entails intense and exhausting exertions. But though the labours of the Absolute might make a great call upon its powers, the most astounding thing about its new activities was the copiousness of its output. Thus, to keep to the department already mentioned, the one solitary tack factory which the Absolute had in its power poured forth night and day so many tacks that they were piled up in mountains in the yard, and eventually broke down the fences and blocked up the street.

Let us stick to this instance of the tacks for the time being. It shows you the whole nature of the Absolute, just as inexhaustible and extravagant as it was at the time of the Creation. Once it had thrown itself into production, it did not trouble about distribution, consumption, market, or ultimate object; it did not trouble about anything: it simply devoted its gigantic energy to pouring forth tacks. Being itself infinite in essence, it knew neither measure nor limitation in anything, even in the matter of tacks.

You can well imagine how the workmen in such a factory were startled by the performances of the new motive power. For them it was a case of wholly unexpected and unfair competition, something that made their labour altogether superfluous; and they would quite rightly have protected themselves against this assault of the capitalism of the Manchester School on the working classes by at least demolishing the factory and hanging its proprietors, if the Absolute had not surprised and overpowered them by its first method of attack, religious illumination of every form and degree. Meantime they experienced levitations, prophecies, miracle-working, visions, supernatural cures, sanctification, love for their neighbours, and other conditions equally unnatural, not to say miraculous.

On the other hand, you can easily guess how the proprietor of such a tack-factory would greet this divine mass-production. He might certainly rejoice, discharge all his workmen, with whom he was in any case well-nigh worried to death, and rub his hands over the volcanic gush of tacks which it cost not a penny to produce. But on the one hand, he himself was sure to fall a victim to the psychic effects of the Absolute, and hand over the whole factory on the spot to his workmen, his brothers in God, as their common property; while on the other hand he very soon realized that those mountains of tacks were utterly valueless because he would find no market for them.

It is true that the workmen no longer had to stand at the machines and carry bars of iron, and were part-proprietors of the factory besides. But in a few days' time it became evident that it was necessary to get rid, somehow or other, of the hundred-ton mountains of tacks which had ceased to be saleable goods. At first some attempts were made to send the tacks off in wagon-loads to imaginary addresses;

later on, there was nothing for it but to cart them off
to huge dumps outside the city. This removal of
the tacks kept all the workmen busy for a full
fourteen hours a day, but they did not grumble,
being illuminated by the divine spirit of love and of
mutual service.

Forgive me for spending so much time over these
tacks. The Absolute was ignorant of industrial
specialization. It invaded the spinning-mills with
equal ardour, and there not only performed the
miracle of making sand into ropes, but even spun it
into thread. In the weaving and fulling mills and
in the stocking factories it laid hold on the entire
textile department, and reeled off without pause
millions of kilometres of everything that can be cut
with scissors. It took possession of the iron works,
the rolling mills, the foundries, the factories for
agricultural machinery, the sawmills, timber works,
rubber works, sugar-mills, chemical works, fertilizer
works, nitrogen and naphtha plants, printing works,
paper-mills, dye works, glass works, potteries, boot
and shoe factories, ribbon works, forges, mines,
breweries, distilleries, creameries, flour-mills, mints,
motor works, and grinding plants. It wove, spun,
knitted, forged, cast, erected, sewed, planed, cut,
dug, burned, printed, bleached, refined, cooked,
filtered, and pressed for twenty-four to twenty-six
hours a day. Harnessed to agricultural machines in

the place of tractors, it ploughed, sowed, harrowed, weeded, cut, harvested and threshed. In every department it augmented the raw material and multiplied the output hundreds of times. It was inexhaustible. It simply squandered its activity. It had found a quantitative expression for its own infinitude: over-production.

The miraculous multiplication of the loaves and fishes in the desert was repeated on a colossal scale in the miraculous multiplication of tacks, boards, nitrates, pneumatic tyres, rolls of paper, and manufactured articles of every kind.

Thus there ruled in the world a state of boundless plenty of all that men could need. But men need everything, everything but boundless plenty.

CHAPTER XV

O F course, in our own orderly and (one might well say) blessed times of general scarcity, we simply cannot imagine the social evil that boundless plenty could be. To us it seems that to find ourselves all of a sudden amid unlimited supplies of everything we wanted would be nothing short of the Earthly Paradise. It would be all to the good, we think; there would be enough of everything for everybody—and Lord! how prices would come down!

Well, then, the economic catastrophe which befell the whole world at the period we are describing, as a result of the interference of the Absolute in industry, arose from the fact that people could get everything they wanted, not merely at a low pirce, but simply for nothing. You might help yourself, free of charge, to a handful of tacks, to go into your boot-soles or into the floor; you could just as easily help yourself to a whole cartload of tacks gratis—only I ask you, what would you do with them? Would you haul them a hundred kilometres off and then give them away? You wouldn't do that; for when you stood before that avalanche of tacks, what you saw was not tacks—relatively useful objects—but something perfectly valueless and senseless in its profusion, something as purposeless as are the stars in the sky. Of course, such a mound of new and shining tacks was often an uplifting sight, and even inspired poetical reflections as do the stars in the sky. They seemed created to be gazed upon in silent wonder. It was a fine sight in its way, as a piece of landscape, just as the sea is from that point of view. But then again, you don't take the sea away in carts into the interior of the country where there is no sea. There is no economic distribution for sea-water —and now there was none for tacks.

And while in one place there spread this sparkling ocean of tacks, in another only a few kilometres farther off there was not a tack to be had. Having become economically worthless, they had disappeared from the shops. If anyone wished to knock one into his shoe or put one into his neighbour's mattress, he sought for it in vain. There weren't any, just as there is no sea at Slaný or Caslav. Where were you then, you business men of days gone by, who used to buy the necessities of life so cheap in one place and sell them so dear in another? Alas, you had vanished, for heavenly grace had descended upon you. You had grown ashamed of your gains; you had shut up your shops to reflect upon the brother-hood of man; you had given away your possessions, and never again would you desire to enrich your-selves by the distribution of those things which are needed by all your brethren in God.

No value means no market. No market means no distribution. No distribution means no goods. And no goods means greater demand, higher prices, bigger profits and larger businesses. And you had turned your backs upon gain and conceived an uncon-trollable antipathy to all figures whatsoever. You had ceased to look upon the material world with the eyes of consumption, market, and sale. You stood with clasped hands staring at the beauty and the profusion of the world. And in the meanwhile the supply of tacks ran out. At last none remained. Only somewhere, far away, they were piled up as by an inexhaustible avalanche.

Even you, ye master bakers, went out in front of your shops, and cried, "Come then, children of God, in the name of Christ, our Master, come and take these loaves and flour and biscuits and rolls. Have pity on us and take them for nothing."

And you, ye drapers, brought your bales of cloth and rolls of linen out into the street, and wept with joy as you cut off five or ten metre lengths for every-one who went by, and begged them for the love of God to accept your little gift; and only when your shop was completely empty of its wares did you fall on your knees and thank God that He had given you the opportunity to clothe your neighbours as He clothes the lilies in the field.

And you, ye butchers and dealers in cooked meats, you took baskets of meat and sausages and polonies on your heads, and went from door to door, and knocked or rang, and begged everybody just to help themselves to whatever they fancied.

And all you who sell boots, furniture, tobacco, bags, spectacles, jewels, carpets, whips, ropes, tin-war, china, books, false teeth, vegetables, medicines, or whatever else one can think of—all of you, touched by the breath of God, poured out into the street, a prey to the generous panic born of grace divine, and gave away all you possessed; after which, either coming together or standing on the threshold of your emptied shops and warehouses, you declared to one another with glowing eyes, "Now, brother, I have eased my conscience."

In a few days it became evident that there was nothing left to give away. But there was also nothing left to buy. The Absolute had pillaged and completely cleaned out every place of business.

Meanwhile, far away from the cities, there poured from the machines millions of metres of wool and linen, Niagaras of lump sugar, all the teeming, magnificent and inexhaustible profusion of the divine over-production of every kind of goods. Some feeble efforts to divide and distribute this flood of commodities were quelled at the outset. It simply could not be mastered.

For that matter, it is possible that this economic catastrophe had also another cause: currency inflation. You see, the Absolute had likewise taken possession of the Government mints and printing establishments, and every day it flung out upon the world hundreds of millions of banknotes, coins, and securities. Utter devaluation was the result: before long a packet of five thousand mark notes meant nothing more than so much waste paper. Whether you offered a halfpenny or half a million for a child's lollypop, it was all the same from the business point of view: you wouldn't get the lollypop, anyhow, for they had all disappeared. Figures had lost all significance. This collapse of the numerical system is, in any case, the natural consequence of the infinitude and omnipotence of God.

At the same time, food shortage and even famine had already made themselves felt in the cities. The organization for the maintenance of supplies had broken down completely for the reasons just mentioned.

Of course there were Ministries of Supply, Commerce, Social Welfare, and Railways, and by our ideas it should have been possible to get control of the gigantic stream of factory production in time, prevent the goods from spoiling, and transport them

carefully to the places which the liberality of the
Absolute had despoiled. Unhappily this plan was
not followed. The personnel of each of the Ministries were the victims of grace in unusual power, and
spent their office hours in joyful prayer. In the
Ministry of Supply a lady clerk named Sarova con-
trolled the situation, preaching on the subject of the
Seven Degrees; in the Ministry of Commerce the
head of a department, Mr. Winkler, proclaimed a
severe asceticism which resembled the teachings of
the Hindu Yoga. True, this excessive zeal lasted
only a fortnight, being succeeded (doubtless through
special inspiration from the Absolute) by a period
of extraordinary devotion to duty. The departments responsible worked feverishly day and night
to avert a breakdown of food supplies, but apparently it was even then too late. The only result was
that each department produced daily from fifteen
to fifty-three thousand bills and enactments, which
by decree of the Inter-Ministerial Commission were
carted away daily on motor lorries to the Vltava
River.

The food situation assuredly offered the most
terrible problem. Luckily, however, there remained
(I am, of course, describing conditions only in our
own country) OUR JOLLY FARMERS. And here,
gentlemen, you must learn that from time immemorial we have had the saying: "With all due

respect to anyone else, our countryfolk are the backbone of the nation." In fact, there's an old rhyme about it, something like this: "Who is the man so strong and tall, Whose daily labour feeds us all? The farmer!"

Who was the man with whom the feverish prodigality of the Absolute came to a halt; who was the man who stood unmoved amid the panic of the markets of the world; who was the man who did not fold his hands in his lap, who did not let himself be carried off his feet, but "remained faithful to the law of his being"? Who was the man so strong and tall whose daily labour fed us all? The farmer!

Yes, it was the farmer (and the same thing happened elsewhere), who by his conduct saved the world from starvation. Just imagine the consequences if he had been seized, like the townsfolk, with the mania for giving everything away to the poor and needy; if he had given away all his corn, his cows and calves, his chickens and geese and potatoes. Within a fortnight famine would have stalked through the cities, and the countryfolk themselves would have been sucked dry, starved out, left stripped of all their supplies. Thanks to our sturdy farmer, this was not to be. Whether you explain it after the event, as being due to the marvellous instinct of the country-dweller, or to his steadfast, pure, deep-rooted tradition, or finally to the fact that in the rural districts the Absolute was less potent, because in the small argricultral holdings the Karburator was not so widely used as in industry— in short, explain it as you please, the fact remains that amid the general collapse of the economic and financial structure, and of the whole market, *the farmer gave nothing away.* He did not give away even a wisp of straw or a grain of oats. Calm and unmoved amid the ruins of the old industrial and commercial order, our farmer went on selling what he had. And he sold it dear. He sensed through some mysterious instinct the calamitous significance of over-production, and so he put on the brakes in time. He did this by raising his prices, however crammed his granaries might be. And it is a testimony to the amazing soundness of the core of our countryfolk that without saying a word to each other, without any organization, led only by the redeeming inward voice, they raised their prices everywhere and for everything. By thus putting up the price of everything, the farmer saved it from destruction. In the midst of insensate profusion he preserved an island of scarcity and costliness. He foresaw, of a surety, that thereby he was saving the world.

For while other goods, being made valueless by being given away gratis, vanished from the market at once as a natural result, foodstuffs continued to be sold. Of course you had to go out into the country to fetch them. The baker and butcher and retailer had nothing they could give you except brotherly love and pious words. So you took up your knapsack and went a hundred and twenty kilometres out. You went from farm to farm, and in one place you bought a kilo of potatoes in exchange for a gold watch, in another an egg for a pair of opera-glasses, in another a kilo of bran for a harmonium or a typewriter. And so you had something to eat. You see, if the farmer had given it all away, you would have been done for long ago. But the farmer saved even a pound of butter for you—of course only in order to dispose of it for a Persian rug or a costly national costume.

Well, who brought the mad communistic experiments of the Absolute to a halt? Who did not lose his head amid the epidemic of righteousness? Who withstood the disastrous tide of superabundance and saved us from destruction without sparing our persons or our purses?

> Who is the man so strong and tall
> Whose daily labour feeds us all?
> The farmer!

CHAPTER XVI

IN THE MOUNTAINS

I<small>T</small> was noon at the Hut in Bear Valley. Rudolf Marek sat curled up on the veranda; he looked at a newspaper, but he soon folded it up again, and gazed out over the far-stretching chain of the Giant Mountains. Stillness, a vast and crystalline stillness, lay upon the mountains, and the man curled up in the chair straightened himself and took a deep breath.

Then the tiny figure of a man appeared from below making towards the Hut.

"How pure the air is here!" thought Marek on his veranda. "Here, Heaven be praised, the Absolute is still latent, it still lies under a spell, hidden in everything, in these mountains and forests, in the sweet grass and the blue sky. Here it does not rush about all over the place, waking terror or working magic; it simply dwells in all matter, a God deeply and quietly present, not even breathing, only in silence watching over all. . . ." Marek clasped his hands in a mute prayer of thankfulness. "Dear God, how pure the air is here!"

The man who had come up from below stopped under the veranda.

"Well, Marek, so I've found you at last!"

Marek looked up, not greatly pleased. The man who stood before him was G. H. Bondy.

"So I've found you at last!" Bondy said again.

"Come along up, then," said Marek, with obvious reluctance. "What the deuce has brought you here? Heavens, man, you do look queer!"

G. H. Bondy did indeed look sunken and yellow; he had gone very grey about the temples, and lines of weariness made dark shadows around his eyes. He seated himself without a word beside Marek and squeezed his hands together between his knees.

"Come now, what's wrong with you?" Marek pressed him after a painful silence.

Bondy raised his arms.

"I'm going to retire, old man. You see, it's got me too . . . *me!*"

"What, religion?" shouted Marek, recoiling as though from a leper.

Bondy nodded. Was it not a tear of shame that trembled on his lashes? Marek whistled softly. "What—it's got you now? My poor old fellow!"

"No," cried Bondy quickly, wiping his eyes. "Don't think I'm not all right at present; I've got under, you might say, Rudy, I've beaten it. But, do you know, when it came over me, it was the very happiest moment of my life. You have no idea, Rudy, what tremendous will-power it takes to shake *that* off."

"I can well believe it," said Marek gravely. "And tell me, what sort of . . . er . . . symptoms did you have?"

"Love for my neighbour," Bondy whispered. "Man, I was frantic with love. I would never have believed it possible to feel anything like it."

There was silence for a moment.

"So, then, you've . . . " Marek began.

"I've thrown it off. Rather like a fox that gnaws its own leg off when it's caught in a trap. But I'm still confoundedly weak after the struggle. An utter wreck, Rudy. As if I'd have typhoid. That's why I've come here, to pick up again, you see. . . . Is it all clear up here?"

"Quite clear; not a single trace of it so far. You can only sense it . . . in Nature and everything; but then one could do that before—one always could, in the mountains."

Bondy kept a gloomy silence. "Well, and what do you make of it all?" he said absently, after a while. "Have you any notion up here of what's going on down below?"

"I get the papers. Even from the papers one can to a certain extent deduce what is happening. Of course these journalists distort everything; still, anyone who can read. . . . I say, Bondy, are things really so awful?"

G. H. Bondy shook his head.

"A lot worse than you think. Simply desperate. Listen," he whispered brokenly. "He's everywhere by now. I think that . . . that He's got a definite plan."

"A plan?" cried Marek, leaping to his feet.

"Don't shout so. He has some kind of plan, my friend. And He's going about it deuced cleverly. Tell me, Marek, what is the greatest power in the world?"

"England," said Marek without hesitation.

"Not at all. Industry is the greatest power in the world. And the so-called 'proletariat' are likewise the greatest power in the world. Do you see the scheme now?"

"No, I don't see it at all."

"He has got control of them both. He has both industry and the masses in His power. So everything is in His grasp. Everything goes to show that He is thinking of world-supremacy. That's how things are, Marek."

Marek sat down. "Wait a bit, Bondy," he said. "I've been thinking a good deal about it up here in the mountains. I've been following up everything and comparing the signs. I tell you, Bondy, I don't even give a thought to anything else. I certainly

don't know what He is aiming at, but I do know
this, Bondy, that He's following no particular plan.
He doesn't know Himself what He wants and how
to get it. Possibly He wants to do something big,
but doesn't know how to set about it. I'll tell you
something, Bondy. So far He's only a force of
Nature. Politically, He's a fearful ignoramus. In
the matter of economics He's a simple savage.
After all, He ought to have submitted to the
Church; she has had experience. . . . You know, He
sometimes strikes me as being so childish. . . ."

"Don't you believe it, Rudy," G. H. Bondy
returned heavily. "He knows what He wants.
That's why He plunged into large-scale industry.
He is far more up to date than we ever thought."

"That is only His play," urged Marek. "He
only wants something to occupy Himself with.
Don't you see, there's a sort of god-like boyishness
about it. Wait, I know what you want to say. As a
worker He is tremendous. It is simply amazing
what He can bring off. But, Bondy, it is so senseless that there can't be any plan in it."

"The most senseless things in history were syste-
matically prosecuted plans," declared G. H. Bondy.

"My dear Bondy," said Marek quickly. "Look at
all the papers I have here. I follow up every step
He takes. I tell you that there isn't a scrap of
consistency about them. They're all merely the

improvisations of omnipotence. He performs tremendous tricks, but at random, disconnectedly, confusedly. His activity isn't organized a scrap. He came into the world altogether too unprepared. That's where His weakness lies. He impresses me, but I see His weak points. He is not a good organizer, and perhaps never has been. He has flashes of genius, but He is unsystematic. I'm surprised that you haven't got the better of Him, Bondy, a wideawake fellow like you."

"You can't do anything with Him," Bondy asserted. "He attacks you in your innermost soul, and you're done for. When He can't convince you by reason, He sends miraculous enlightenment upon you. You know what He did with Saul."

"You are running away from Him," said Marek, "but I am running after Him, and I'm close at His heels. I know a bit about Him already, enough to get out a warrant for Him! Description: infinite, invisible, and formless. Place of residence: everywhere in the vicinity of atomic motors. Occupation: mystical Communism. Crimes for which He is wanted: alienation of private property, illegal practice of medicine, offences against the Public Assemblies Act, interference with officials in the execution of their duty, and so forth. Distinguishing marks: omnipotence. In short, have Him arrested."

"You're making fun of it," sighed G. H. Bondy. "Don't do it. He has beaten us."

"Not yet!" cried Marek. "Look here, Bondy. He doesn't know how to govern yet. He has got into a fearful muddle with His new undertakings. For instance, He has gone in for over-production instead of first building up a miraculous railway system. Now He's in the mire Himself—what He produces has no value. That miraculous profusion of everything was a fearful fiasco. In the second place, He turned the brains of the authorities with His mysticism and upset the whole machinery of Government, which otherwise He could now be using to maintain order. You can make revolutions anywhere else you like, but not in the Government offices; even if the world's to be brought to an end, the thing to do is to destroy the universe first and take the Government offices afterwards. That's how it is, Bondy. And in the third place, like the crudest of doctrinaire Communists, He has done away with the currency and thereby with one stroke paralysed the circulation of commodities. He did not know that the laws of the market are stronger than the laws of God. He did not know that production without trade is utterly senseless. He knew nothing whatever. He behaved like . . . like a . . . well, to put it shortly, as if He would destroy with one hand what He made with the other. Here we have miraculous profusion, and along with it disastrous shortage. He is all-powerful, yet He's achieved only chaos. I believe that He once did really create the laws of Nature, the primordial lizards, the mountains, and anything else you like. But business, Bondy, our modern industry and commerce, that I swear He did not create, for He simply doesn't know a thing about it. No, Bondy, industry and commerce are not of God."

"Hold on," said G. H. Bondy. "I know that the consequences of His acts are calamitous . . . immeasurable. . . . But what can we do about it?"

"For the time being, nothing. My dear Bondy, I just study and compare. It is a second Babel. Here, for instance, you have the Roman Catholic publications expressing the suspicion that 'the confusions of these times of religious excitement are being deliberately organized with Satanic subtlety by the Freemasons.' The Nationalist Press blames the Jews, the Socialists of the Right blame those of the Left, the Agrarian party attacks the Liberals; it's killing. And mind you, we're not really in the whirlpool yet. In my opinion, the whole thing is only just beginning to get into a tangle. Come here, Bondy, I want to tell you something."

"Well?"

"Do you think that He . . . you know what I mean . . . that He's the only one there is?"

"I don't know," replied Bondy. "And is it of any special importance?"

"Immense importance," Marek answered. "Come closer, Bondy, and prick up your ears."

CHAPTER XVII

THE HAMMER AND STAR

"BROTHER SENIOR WARDEN, what do you see in the East?" asked the Worshipful Master. He was dressed all in black, wore the white leather apron, and held the silver gavel in his hand.

"I see the Masters assembled in the Temple and ready for labour," said the Senior Warden.

The Worshipful Master gave a knock with his gavel.

"Brother Junior Warden, what do you see in the West?"

"I see the Masters assembled in the Temple and ready for labour."

The Worshipful Master knocked three times with his gavel. "Let the labour begin."

The Brothers of the Free French Masonic Lodge, "The Hammer and Star," took their seats, never taking their eyes off the Worshipful Master, G. H. Bondy, who had called them together at such an unusual time. The lodge was as quiet as a church between the black-draped walls with the maxims of the craft woven in the hangings. Bondy, the Worshipful Master, was pale and thoughtful.

"Brothers," said the Worshipful Master after a while, "I have summoned this unusual meeting . . . for this . . . er . . . unusual labour, which in . . . er . . . unusual opposition to the secret precepts of our Order . . . is no mere formality. I know . . . that I am violating the solemn and consecrated form of our labour . . . in asking you to come to a decision upon . . . a really serious . . . and public matter . . . of the highest importance."

"The Worshipful Master in the Chair has the right to order our labour," declared the Judex Formidabilis, causing general agitation among his hearers.

"Well, then," began G. H. Bondy, "it concerns the systematic attacks . . . upon our Order recently begun . . . by the Clerical party. They state that our secret activities . . . of the last hundred years . . . are connected with certain extraordinary . . . and regrettable occurrences . . . in the industrial and spiritual field. The Clericalist papers assert that the Masonic Lodges . . . have brought about . . . deliberately . . . this unfettering of demoniacal powers. I ask you . . . what we ought to do . . . in the present time of calamity . . . for the benefit of mankind . . . and for the honour of the Most High. This subject is now open for discussion."

After a moment's solemn silence the Junior Warden arose.

"Brothers, at this historic moment, I welcome, so to speak, the impressive words uttered by our Worshipful Master. He spoke, so to speak, of regrettable occurrences. And indeed, we who concern ourselves, so to speak, only with the welfare of mankind, are bound to declare all these regrettable miracles, illuminations, fits of love for one's neighbour, and other disturbances to be occurrences which are, so to speak, in the highest degree regrettable. We must with all the discretion we owe to our Order decline all connection, so to speak, with these regrettable facts which, so to speak, do not agree with the traditional and progressive principles of our Great Order. Brothers, these regrettable principles are, so to speak, in fundamental disagreement with it, as our Worshipful Master very rightly said, since the Clericals, so to speak, have taken up arms against us, and if we have in mind, so to speak, the highest interests of mankind. I therefore move that we should express our agreement in the fullest sense of the word, as the Worshipful Master in the Chair very rightly said, these regrettable occurrences."

Judex Formidabilis now rose.

"Brother Worshipful Master, I should like to say a few words. I have to observe that certain occurrences have been spoken of here in a very regrettable manner. I am of opinion that those occurrences are not so regrettable as our Brother Junior Warden thinks. I am really not aware which occurrences Brother Junior Warden is alluding to, but if he has in mind the religious meetings which I myself attend, then I am of the opinion that he is mistaken. Indeed, I will say frankly that I consider that he is entirely in error."

"I move," suggested another brother, "that we should take a vote on whether the said occurrences are regrettable or not."

"And I move," said another, taking the floor, "that we elect a smaller committee, of some three members, say, to investigate these regrettable occurrences."

"I am in favour of five members."

"I vote for twelve."

Judex Formidabilis was heard to say, "Excuse me, brothers, I have not yet finished speaking."

The Worshipful Master rapped with his gavel.

"I call upon Brother Judex Formidabilis."

"Brothers," began Judex gently, "we will not quarrel who is to have the floor. The occurrences concerning which several regrettable opinions have been expressed here are of a character that deserves attention, interest, yes, and even respect. I do not deny that I am a member of several religious circles who have received divine grace in especial power. I trust that this is not inconsistent with the discipline of the Freemason."

"Not at all," said several voices.

"Moreover, I have to admit that I myself have been priviliged to perform a few minor miracles. I think that this does not conflict with my rank and degree."

"Certainly not."

"May I therefore, speaking from my own experiences, state that the aforesaid occurrences are, on the contrary, praiseworthy, uplifting, and moral, that they contribute to the welfare of mankind and the glory of the Most High, and therefore—from the Masonic standpoint—there can be no objection to them. I move that our Lodge should declare its neutrality with respect to all these manifestations of the divine presence."

The Senior Warden rose and said: "Brothers, I certainly don't believe in any of this stuff, and I've seen nothing of it; all the same I'm in favour of standing up for religion. I don't think that there's anything in it, but is there any reason why we should say so? I therefore move that we secretly let it be known that we have the very best information about the whole business, and that we approve of things going on as they are."

The Worshipful Master raised his eyes and said: "I call the attention of the brethren to the fact that the Industrial Federation has elected the Absolute as its honorary President. Further, that the M.E.C.

shares, the so-called Absolute Stock, may go up still higher. In this connection I may say that a donor who wishes to remain unknown has contributed one thousand shares to the Benevolent Fund of our Lodge. The meeting will now proceed."

The Junior Warden announced: "I beg to withdraw, so to speak, the regrettable occurrences. From the higher point of view I entirely agree. I move that we discuss the matter from the higher point of view."

The Worshipful Master raised his eyes and said: "I have to inform you that the Grand Lodge intends to issue instructions relating to the recent occurrences. The Grand Lodge recommends the Masters to join religious circles and organize them in the Masonic sense for the instruction of apprentices in the craft. The new Temples are to be conducted in an enlightened and anticlerical spirit. It is desirable to examine the various doctrines—monism, abstinence, Fletcherism, vegetarianism, and so forth. Each circle is to be instructed in a different faith in order to test out practically which is the best for the welfare of mankind and for the glory of the Most High. These activities are obligatory on all Masters by decree of the Grand Lodge. The meeting will now proceed."

CHAPTER XVIII

THE largest Catholic or popular newspaper, *The People's Friend,* had not a very large editorial staff, and so at 9.30 p. m. there were only two men in the room—Kostal, the night editor (Heaven knows why night editors' pipes have such an amazing stink), and Father Jost, who sat writing the leader for the next issue and whistling between his teeth.

At that moment Novotny, the printer, came in with the wet proofs.

"Well, how about the leader, gentlemen, the leader?" he growled. "When are we going to set it?"

Father Jost stopped humming. "Ready in a minute, Novotny," he said quickly. "There's just a word I can't get. Have we already had 'satanic machinations'?"

"The day before yesterday."

"Aha. And has 'treacherous onslaught' been used too?"

"Yes, we've had that."

" 'Knavish imposture'?"

144

"We ran that to-day."

" 'Impious fabrication' ?"

"At least six times," said Kostal.

"That's a pity," sighed Father Jost. "I think we've been a bit too lavish with our ideas. How did you like to-day's leader, Novotny?"

"Strong stuff," said the printer. "But we ought to be getting on with the setting."

"Ready in a minute," Father Jost replied. "I think our friends in higher quarters were satisfied with this morning's issue. You'll see, his Lordship the Bishop will call on us. 'Jost,' he'll say, 'you let them have it properly.' Have we used 'maniacal ravings' ?"

"Yes."

"What a pity! We must bring up fresh guns and blaze away. 'Jost,' his Lordship said to me not long ago, 'Up and at them! Everything may have its day, but we shall stand for ever and aye.' Mr. Novotny, can't you think of any suitable phrase?"

"Well, couldn't you say 'criminal narrow-mindedness' or 'perverse malignity'?"

"That would do splendidly," said Father Jost, with a sigh of relief. "Where do you get all these bright ideas from, Novotny?"

"From the old files of *The People's Friend*. But that leader, your Reverence."

"You shall have it at once. Just wait a minute:

'The criminal narrow-mindedness or perverse malignity which with the idolatries of Baal sullies the pure waters from the rock of Peter!—aha, now we shan't be long—sullies the pure waters, rock of Peter, there we are—and sets up thereon the golden calf whose name is the Devil or the Absolute—' "

"Have you got the leader?" came a voice from the door of the night editor's room.

"*Laudetur Jesus Christus,* my Lord Bishop," ejaculated Father Jost.

"Have you got the leader?" repeated Bishop Linda, coming hurriedly into the room. "Who was it that wrote this morning's leader? Heaven forgive me, what a pretty mess you've made with it. What idiot wrote it?"

"I . . . I did," stammered Father Jost, retreating; "Bishop . . . Your Lordship . . . I thought . . ."

"You've no right to think," roared Bishop Linda, his eyeglasses flashing at him eerily. "Here, take the thing"; and crumpling up that morning's issue of *The People's Friend* in his hand, he flung it at Jost's feet. "I thought! Look at him, he thinks! Why didn't you telephone? Why didn't you ask what you were to write? And you, Kostal, how could you put it in the paper? You thought, too, did you? Novotny!"

"Yes, sir," exclaimed the trembling printer.

"Why did you have that stuff set up in type? Did you think, too?"

"Oh, no, sir," protested the printer. "I have to set what they send me. . . ."

"Nobody has to do anything but what I want," Bishop Linda declared decisively. "Jost, sit down and read the drivel you put together this morning. Read it, I tell you."

"For a long time past," Father Jost read, in trembling tones, from his own leading article—"for a long time past the public has been disturbed by the knavish imposture . . ."

"What?"

"Knavish imposture, my lord," groaned Father Jost. "I thought—I—I see now . . ."

"What do you see?"

"That 'knavish imposture' is a little too forcible."

"So I should think. Read on!"

". . . knavish imposture carried on with the so-called Absolute . . . by means of which the Freemasons, the Jews and other progressives are befooling the world. It has been scientifically demonstrated . . ."

"Look at Jost! Look at him!" cried Bishop Linda. "He has scientifically demonstrated something! Read on."

". . . scientifically demonstrated," stammered the unfortunate Jost, "that the so-called Absolute

. . . is just as impious a deception . . . as the tricks performed by mediums. . . ."

"Stop," said the Bishop with a sudden amiability. "Take down the following leading article: 'It has been scientifically demonstrated . . .' Have you got that? . . . 'demonstrated that I, Father Jost, am a jackass, a dolt and an idiot.' . . . Have you got that?"

"Yes," whispered Jost, utterly bewildered. "Please go on, my . . . my lord."

"Throw that into the waste-paper basket, my son," said the Bishop, "and open your stupid ears. Have you read to-day's papers?"

"Yes, my l . . ."

"Ah, well, I don't know. This morning, my reverend fried, there appeared first of all a communication from the Monist Association, asserting that the Absolute is that Unity which the Monists have always proclaimed to be God, and that therefore the cult of the Absolute is in complete correspondence with the doctrine of Monism. Did you read that?"

"Yes."

"There was also the announcement that the Masonic Lodges commend the Absolute to the support of their members. Did you read that?"

"Yes."

"Further, that at the Synodical Congress of the

Lutherans, Superintendent Maartens gave a five-hour address in which he proved the identity of the Absolute with God made manifest. Did you read that?"

"Yes."

"Also that at the convention of the Seventh International the Russian delegate, Paruskin-Rebenfeld, moved that honour should be paid to Comrade God who had proved His sympathy for the workers by entering the factories. It had been noted with gratitude that the Most High Comrade had decided to work in place of the expropriated classes. A motion was brought forward that as a further proof of solidarity He should begin a general strike in all His undertakings. After the presiding officers had deliberated in private, the motion was recalled as premature. Did you read that?"

"Yes."

"Finally a resolution was passed that the Absolute was the exclusive property of the proletariat, and that the bourgeoise had no right to do honour to Him or to benefit by His miracles. Instructions were given to devise a scheme for a workers' cult of the Absolute and to carry out secret defensive measures in case capital should attempt to exploit or appropriate the Absolute. Did you read that?"

"Yes."

"There also appeared an announcement by the

Free Thought Society, a notice sent in by the Salvation Army, a communiqué from the Theosophical Centre 'Adyar,' an open letter addressed to the Absolute and signed by the Benevolent Association of Landlords, an announcement by the Federation of Merry-Go-Round Proprietors, signed by the President, J. Binder, besides *The Voice of the Union of Constance,* special numbers of the *Voice from the Beyond,* the *Anabaptist Reader* and the *Abstainer*—did you read all that, my friend?"

"Yes."

"Well, then, my dear son, you see this: that in every case they make the most solemn claim that the Absolute is their own private property, they do Him honour, and make Him splendid offers, appoint Him honorary member, patron, protector, and Heaven knows what else—and meanwhile on our side some crazy lunatic of a Father Jost—Jost, if you please, an insignificant object called Jost—shouts out to the universe that it's all a knavish imposture and a swindle already scientifically exposed. Saints and martyrs, you've got us into a pretty fix!"

"But, my lord, I had orders to . . . write against those phenomena . . ."

"So you had," the Bishop interrupted him sternly. "But didn't you see that the situation had entirely changed? Jost," cried the Bishop, rising to his feet, "our churches are empty, our flock is running after the Absolute. Jost, you blockhead, if we wish to bring our flock back to us, we must secure the Absolute. We will set up Atomic Karburators in all our churches . . . but that, my little priest, is above your head. Bear in mind this one thing: the Absolute must work for us; He must be ours, i.e. He must be ours alone. *Capiscis, mi fili?*"

"*Capisco,*" whispered Father Jost.

"*Deo gratias!* Now, friend Jost, now shall Saul become Paul. You'll write a nice little leading article in which you will make it known that the Sacred Congregation, taking cognizance of the petitions of the faithful, has admitted the Absolute into the bosom of the Church. Mr. Novotny, here is the Apostolic Letter to that effect; have it set up in large bold type on the front page of the paper. Kostal, announce among the local news items that Mr. G. H. Bondy will on Sunday next receive the sacrament of baptism at the hands of the Archbishop, and add a few words of hearty welcome, of course, you understand? And you, Jost, sit down and write. . . . Wait a minute; we want something really striking to lead off with."

"We might say something after this style, my lord: "The criminal narrow-mindedness and the perverse malignity of certain bodies . . .""

"Splendid! Then say: 'The criminal narrow-mindedness and the perverse malignity of certain bodies have for some months past been active in endeavouring to mislead our people into the paths of error. False and heretical doctrines have been proclaimed to the effect that the Absolute is something other than the selfsame God to whom we have from the cradle raised our hands.' . . . Have you got that? . . . 'raised our hands in childlike faith . . . and love.' . . . Have you got that? Continue . . ."

CHAPTER XIX

THE PROCESS OF CANONIZATION

YOU will readily understand that the admission
of the Absolute to the bosom of the Church
afforded, under the given circumstances, a great
surprise. It was carried out by virtue of the Papal
Brief alone, and the College of Cardinals, being
faced with the accomplished fact, merely deliberated
whether the sacrament of baptism should be con-
ferred upon the Absolute. It was decided to dispense
with this. There was certainly well-known ecclesiastical precedent for the baptism of a God (*vide* John
the Baptist); but even in such a case the candidate
for baptism must be present in person. Besides,
it was a very delicate political question to decide
which reigning potentate was to be godfather to the
Absolute. The Sacred Congregation therefore
recommended that at the next Pontifical Mass the
Holy Father should pray for the new member of
the Church, and this was duly carried out in very
solemn form. It was also made part of the body of
Church doctrine that in addition to the sacrament of
baptism and baptism by blood the Church also

recognized baptism through works of meritoriousness, and virtue.

It must also be recorded that three days before the publication of the Papal Brief the Pope gave a lengthy audience to G. H. Bondy, who was afterwards in conference with the Papal Secretary, Monsignor Cullatti, for twenty-four hours.

Almost simultaneously the summary beatification of the Absolute was enacted under the rule *super cultu immemorabili* in recognition of the virtuous life of the Absolute, now declared Blessed, and a regular but expedited process of canonization was arranged for. There was, however, one highly important innovation: the Absolute was to be declared, not a Saint, but a God. A Deification Commission was immediately appointed from among the best of the Church's scholars and pastors. Varesi, the Cardinal Archbishop of Venice, was appointed Procurator Dei, while Monsignor Cullatti was to act as Advocatus Diaboli.

Cardinal Varesi presented seventeen thousand testimonies to miracles performed, signed by nearly all the cardinals, patriarchs, primates, metropolitans, princes of the Church, archbishops, principals of Orders, and abbots. To each testimonial were appended expert reports by medical authorities and members of faculties, opinions from professors of natural sciences, technicians, and economists, as well

as the signatures of eye-witnesses and legal authenti-
cations. These seventeen thousand documents,
Monsignor Varesi stated, represented but an insignificant fraction of the miracles actually performed
by the Absolute, their number having already at a
conservative estimate exceeded thirty millions.

In addition to this the Procurator Dei secured
detailed expert opinions from the greatest scientific
specialists in the world. Professor Gardien, Rector
of the medical faculty in Paris, for example, after
exhaustive researches, wrote as follows: "Seeing
that innumerable cases presented to us for examination were from a medical standpoint completely
hopeless and scientifically incurable (paralysis, can-
cer of the throat, blindness after surgical removal of
both eyes, lameness following on amputation of both
the lower extremities, death following on complete
separation of the head from the trunk, strangulation
in a subject hanged two days before, etc.), the
medical faculty of the Sorbonne is of the opinion
that the so-called miraculous cures in such cases can
only be ascribed either to complete ignorance of
anatomical and pathological conditions, clinical inex-
perience, and utter incompetence in medical practice,
or—a possibility we do not wish to exclude—to the
interference of higher powers not limited by the
laws of nature or any knowledge thereof."

Professor Meadow of Glasgow, the psychologist,

wrote: ". . . . Since in these activities there is manifest what is obviously a thinking being, capable of association, memory, and even of logical judgment, a being which performs these psychic operations without the medium of a brain and nervous system, it affords a striking corroboration of my crushing criticism of the psychophysical parallelism advocated by Professor Meyer. I affirm that the so-called Absolute is a psychic, conscious, and intelligent being, albeit our scientific knowledge of its nature is as yet but small."

Professor Lupen of the Brno Technical Institute wrote: "From the standpoint of effective performance, the Absolute is a force deserving of the highest respect."

The famous chemist, Willibald of Tubingen, wrote: "The Absolute possesses all the requisite conditions of existence and scientific evolution, as it is in admirable conformity with Einstein's theory of Relativity."

The present chronicler will no longer detain you with the pronouncements of the world's scientific luminaries; in any case they were all published in the Acts of the Holy See.

The process of canonization went forward in quick time. In the meantime a committee of eminent authorities on dogma and exegesis had completed a statement in which the identity of the Absolute with the Third Person of the Trinity was definitely established on the basis of the Scriptures and the writings of the Fathers of the Church.

But before the ceremony of deification took place, the Patriarch of Constantinople declared, as head of the Eastern Church, the identity of the Absolute with the First Person of the Trinity, the Creator. This undeniably heretical teaching was espoused by the Old Catholics, the circumcised Christians of Abyssinia, the Evangelicals of the Helvetian Confession, the Nonconformists, and several of the larger American sects. This brought about a lively theological dispute. As for the Jews, a secret doctrine spread among them to the effect that the Absolute was Baal of old; the Liberal Jews announced that they would in that case recognize Baal.

The Free Thought Society assembled in Basle. In the presence of two thousand delegates the Absolute was proclaimed as the God of the Freethinkers, and this was followed by an incredibly violent attack upon clerics of all denominations, who, in the terms of the resolution, "are eager to seek their own advantage with the one scientific God and to drag Him down into the filthy cage of ecclesiastical dogma and priestly deception, and leave Him there to starve." But the God who has made Himself manifest to the eyes of every progressive modern thinker "has nothing to do with the mediæval traffic of these

Pharisees; the Free Thought Association alone is His congregation, and only the Basle Congress has the right to set forth the doctrine and the ritual of the Free Religion."

At about the same time the German Monist Association laid in Leipzig, with great pomp and ceremony, the foundation-stone of the future Cathedral of the Atomic God. There was some disturbance, in which sixteen persons were injured and Lüttgen, the famous physicist, had his spectacles smashed.

News was also received that autumn of some religious phenomena in the Belgian Congo and in French Senegambia. The negroes quite unexpectedly slaughtered and ate the missionaries and bowed down to a new idol which they called Ato or Alolto. It afterwards appeared that these idols were atomic motors, and that German officers and agents were in some way implicated in the matter. On the other hand, during the Moslem rising which broke out at Mecca in December of the same year, several French emissaries were found to have been present, who had concealed twelve light atomic motors of the Aero pattern in the neighbourhood of the Kaaba. The ensuing rebellion of the Mohammedans in Egypt and Tripoli, and the massacres in Arabia, cost the lives of about thirty thousand Europeans.

The deification of the Absolute was at length

accomplished in Rome on the twelfth of December.

Seven thousand priests with lighted candles escorted the Holy Father to St. Peter's, where the largest twelve-ton Karburator, a gift from the M.E.C. to the Holy See, had been erected behind the high altar. The ceremony lasted five hours, and twelve hundred of the faithful and the spectators were crushed to death. At the stroke of noon, the Pope intoned the "In nomine Dei Deus," and at the same moment the bells of all the Catholic churches in the world were set ringing as all the bishops and priests turned from the altars and announced to the world of believers: "Habemus Deum."

CHAPTER XX

S<small>T</small>. K<small>ILDA</small> is a little island, practically nothing more than a rock of pliocene tufa far to the west of the Hebrides. A few stunted birches, a handful of heather and dry grass, flocks of nesting seagulls and semi-arctic butterflies of the order *Polyommatus* are all that lives on this lost outpost of our hemisphere, out amid the endless beating of the seas and the equally endless procession of clouds for ever laden with rain. For that matter, St. Kilda has always been uninhabited, is now, and will for ever be so.

Nevertheless it was there that His Majesty's ship *Dragon* dropped anchor, towards the end of autumn. Carpenters came off the ship with timbers and planks, and by evening they had built a large, low wooden house. The next day upholsterers arrived, bringing with them the finest and most comfortable furniture. On the third day stewards, cooks, and waiters emerged from the depths of the ship and carried into the building crockery, wine, preserves, and everything that civilization has provided for rich, fastidious, and powerful men.

On the morning of the fourth day there arrived on H.M.S. *Edwin* the English Premier, the Right Hon. Sir W. O'Patterney; half an hour later came the American Ambassador, Mr. Horatio Bumm; and there followed him, each on a warship, the Chinese plenipotentiary, Mr. Kei; the French Premier, Dudieu; the Imperial Russian General, Buchtin; the Imperial German Chancellor, Dr. Wurm; the Italian Minister, Prince Trivelino; and the Japanese Ambassador, Baron Yanato. Sixteen English torpedo-boats cruised around St. Kilda to prevent newspaper reporters from landing; for this Conference of the Supreme Council of the Great Powers, which had been summoned in great haste by the all-powerful Sir W. O'Patterney, was to take place under conditions of the strictest secrecy. In fact, the large Danish whaling schooner *Nyls Hans* was torpedoed while attempting to slip through the cordon of destroyers by night. The losses included, in addition to the twelve men of the crew, Mr. Joe Hashek, political correspondent of the *Chicago Tribune*. Nevertheless, the representative of the *New York Herald*, Mr. I. Sawitt, spent the whole time on St. Kilda disguised as a waiter, and we are indebted to his pen for the scanty accounts of that memorable assembly which survived even the subsequent historic catastrophes.

Mr. I. Sawitt was of the opinion that this Conference on high politics was being held in this lonely spot in order to eliminate any direct influence of the Absolute on its decisions. In any other place the Absolute might well make its way into this gathering of serious statesmen in the guise of inspiration, enlightenment, or even miracle-working—which would certainly be something utterly unprecedented in high politics.

The primary purpose of the Conference was ostensibly to reach an agreement on colonial policy. The States were to come to an agreement not to support or assist religious movements on the territory of other States. The incentive to this step was the German agitation in the Congo and Senegambia, as well as the subterranean French influence behind the outbreak of Mahdism in Moslem countries under British rule, and particularly the shipments of Karburators from Japan to Bengal, where a furious revolt of the most diverse sects was raging.

The deliberations were held behind closed doors. The only news given out for publication was that spheres of interest had been allotted to Germany in Kurdistan and to Japan on certain Greek islands. It would seem that the Anglo-Japanese and the Franco-German-Russian alliances were on this occasion unusually cordial.

In the afternoon Mr. G. H. Bondy arrived on a

special torpedo-boat, and was received in audience by the Supreme Council.

Not until about five o'clock (Greenwich time) did the illustrious diplomats sit down to luncheon, and it was here that I. Sawitt had the first opportunity of hearing with his own ears the representatives of the high contracting parties. After the meal they discussed sport and actresses. Sir W. O'Patterney, with his poet's head with its white mane and soulful eyes, talked enthusiastically about salmon-fishing with His Excellency the French Premier, Dudieu, whose energetic gestures, loud voice, and a certain *je ne sais quoi,* revealed the former lawyer. Baron Yanato, refusing all liquid refreshment, listened silently and smiled as though his mouth were full of water. Dr. Wurm turned over his papers, General Buchtin walked up and down the room with Prince Trivelino, Horatio Bumm was making cannons all by himself on the billiard-table (I have myself seen his lovely overhand massé stroke, which would win the admiration of any expert), while Mr. Kei, looking like a very yellow and very withered old lady, fingered some kind of Buddhist rosary. He was a mandarin in his own Flowery Land.

Suddenly all the diplomats grouped themselves round M. Dudieu, who was explaining: "Yes, gentlemen, *c'est ca.* We cannot remain indifferent to Him. We must either recognize Him or deny

Him. We Frenchmen are in favour of the latter course!"

"That's because He's showing himself such an anti-militarist in your country," said Prince Trivelino with a certain malicious pleasure.

"No, gentlemen," cried Dudieu, "don't deceive yourselves on that point. The French army is quite unaffected. Such an anti-militarist! Bah! We already had any number of anti-militarist! Beware of Him, gentlemen. He is a demagogue, a communist, a bigot, Heaven knows what not, but always a radical. *Oui, un rabouliste, c'est ca.* He sticks to the wildest popular catch-words. He goes with the mob. Now in your Highness's country"—he turned suddenly to Prince Trivelino—"He is a nationalist, intoxicating Himself with dreams of a great Roman Empire. But take care, your Highness: that's what He does in the cities, but in the country districts He hobnobs with the parsons and performs miracles at the shrines of the Virgin. He works for the Vatican with one hand and for the Quirinal with the other. Either there is some design in it or . . . I don't know what. Gentlemen, we can quite frankly admit it: He is making things difficult for us all."

"In my country," said Horatio Bumm thoughtfully, leaning on his cue, "He goes in for sport as well. He's a real big sportsman. He goes in for all sorts of games. He's made amazing records in sports even among chapel-folk. He's a Socialist. He's on the side of the Wets. He changes water into drink. Why, just lately, at a White House banquet, everybody present, everybody, mind you, got frightfully drunk. They didn't take anything but water, you see, but He changed it into drink after it was down."

"That's queer," said Sir W. O'Patterney. "In my country He strikes one as much more of a Conservative. He behaves like an omnipotent clergyman. Holds meetings, processions, sermons in the streets, and such things. I think He is opposed to us Liberals.

Baron Yanato then said smilingly: "In my country He is quite at home. A very, very nice God. He has adapted Himself very well. Indeed, a very great Japanese."

"What do you mean, Japanese?" croaked out General Buchtin. "What are you talking about, batushko? He's a Russian, a genuine Russian, a Slav. With the great Russian soul, your Excellency. He's on the side of us moujiks. Not long ago our Archimandrite arranged a procession in his honour: ten thousand candles, and people, gospodin, thick as poppy seeds. All the Christian souls of Mother Russia had gathered together for it. He even per-

formed miracles for us. For He is our Father,"
added the General, crossing himself and bowing
low.

The German Imperial Chancellor approached,
and after listening for a while in silence, he said:
"Yes, He knows just how to appeal to the people.
In every case, He adopts the mentality of the country
He is in. Considering His age, He is . . . hm . . .
astoundingly elastic. We notice it in the countries
just around us. In Czechoslovakia, for instance, He
behaves like a colossal individualist. Everyone there
has his own Absolute all to himself, so to speak. We
ourselves have a State Absolute. With us the
Absolute immediately developed into the higher consciousness of the State. In Poland He acts like a
kind of alcohol; with us He acts like . . . like . . .
a sort of Higher Command, *verstehen sie mich?*"

"Even in your Catholic provinces?" asked Prince
Trivelino with a smile.

"Those are mere local differences," replied Dr.
Wurm. "Don't attach any importance to them,
gentlemen. Germany is more united that ever before. But I must thank you, Prince, for the Catholic
Karburators that you are smuggling over to us.
Fortunately they are poorly made, like all Italian
products."

"Come, come, gentlemen," interrupted Sir W.
O'Patterney. "Neutrality in religious questions,

please. For my own part, I use a double hook for salmon. The other day I caught one as long as that, look! Fourteen pounds."

"And what about the Papal Nuncio?" asked Dr. Wurm quietly.

"The Holy See requests us to maintain order at all costs. It wants us to have mysticism prohibited by the police. That wouldn't do in England, and altogether. . . . Well, I assure you it weighed quite fourteen pounds. Heavens, I had all I could do to keep from falling into the water!"

Baron Yanato smiled still more politely. "But we do not wish for neutrality. He is a great Japanese. The whole world can adopt the Japanese faith. We, too, would like to send out missionaries for once, and teach religion."

"Baron," said Sir W. O'Patterney gravely, "you know that the excellent relations existing between our Governments . . ."

"England can adopt the Japanese faith," smiled Baron Yanato, "and our relations will be even better."

"Stop, batushko," cried General Buchtin. "We'll have no Japanese faith. If there's to be any faith, then it must be the Orthodox faith. And do you know why? First, because it is orthodox, and secondly, because it is Russian, and thirdly, because our Czar so wills it, and fourthly, because we, my friend, have the biggest army. I do everything like a soldier, gentlemen: downright frankly and openly. If there's to be a religion, then it's to be our Orthodox religion."

"But, gentlemen, that is not the question," cried Sir W. O'Patterney excitedly. "That isn't what we're here for!"

"Quite right," said Dr. Wurm. "We have to agree upon a common line of conduct with regard to God."

"Which one?" suddenly asked the Chinese plenipotentiary, Mr. Kei, lifting at last his wrinkled eyelids.

"Which one?" repeated Dr. Wurm in astonishment. "Why, surely there's only one."

"Our Japanese God," smiled Baron Yanato blandly.

"The Orthodox Greek God, batushko, and none other," contradicted the General, as red in the face as a turkey-cock.

"Buddha," Mr. Kei said, and again dropped his lids, becoming the very counterpart of a dried-up mummy.

Sir W. O'Patterney stood up agitatedly. "Gentlemen," he said, "kindly follow me."

Thereupon the diplomats again proceeded to the council chamber. At eight o'clock in the evening His Excellency, General Buchtin, rushed out, purple in the face, and clenching his fists. After him came Dr. Wurm, agitatedly arranging his papers. Sir W. O'Patterney, regardless of polite usage, came out with his hat on his head: his face was deep red; M. Dudieu followed him in silence. Prince Trivelino walked away looking very pale, Baron Yanato at his heels with his perpetual smile. The last to leave was Mr. Kei, with downcast eyes, an exceedingly long black rosary sliding through his fingers.

This concludes the report which I. Sawitt published in the *Herald*. No official communication concerning this Conference was given out, except the one already mentioned relating to the spheres of interest, and if any decision was taken it was apparently of no great value. For already, to use the familiar gynæcological phrase, unforeseen events were shaping themselves in the "womb of history."

CHAPTER XXI

THE TELEGRAM

SNOW was falling in the mountains. All night through it had come down in great silent flakes; nearly two feet deep of it lay there new-fallen, and still the white starlets of snow floated earthwards without a pause.

Silence lay over the forests, save that now and then a branch would snap beneath too great a load, and the sound would drive itself a little path through the stillness intensified by the snow.

Then it grew colder, and from the direction of Prussia came whistling an icy wind. The soft flakes changed into stinging hail hurling itself straight into your face. The fallen snow rose in sharp needle-points and whirled through the air. White clouds blew down from the trees, swirled madly above the ground, spun about, and soared up to the darkened heavens. It was snowing upwards from the earth to the sky.

In the depths of the forest the branches were creaking and groaning; a tree broke and fell with a crash, shattering the undergrowth. But abrupt noises like these were sundered and swept away on the whistling, booming, shrieking, rending, distracted howl of the wind. When for an instant it ceased, you could hear the frozen snow crunching shrilly under your feet like powdered glass.

Above Spindelmühl a telegraph messenger was making his way through the storm. It was confoundedly heavy going through the heaped-up snow. The messenger had his cap fastened tight over his ears with a red handkerchief, and had woollen gloves on, and a gaudy scarf round his neck, and still he was cold. "Ah, well," he was thinking, "in another hour and a half at any rate I'll have crawled up to Bear Valley, and I'll borrow a sledge for the run down. But what the devil possesses people to send telegrams in filthy weather like this!"

At the Maiden's Bridge a gust caught him and spun him round nearly in a circle. With frozen hands he clung to the post of the signboard set there for tourists. "Holy Virgin!" he muttered, "this surely can't last!" And then across a clearing a huge cloud-like mass of snow came whirling towards him—coming nearer and nearer—now down upon him . . . he must hold his breath at all costs. . . . A thousand needle-points drove into his face and made their way inside his coat; through a little rent in his clothing the icy particles reached his skin; the man was drenched beneath his frozen garments. The cloud blew past, and the messenger felt very much disposed to turn back to the post-office.

"Marek, Engineer"—he repeated the address to himself. "Well, he certainly don't belong to these parts. But a telegram's urgent, you never know what it's about—one of his family, maybe, or something important. . . ."

The storm calmed down a little, and the messenger struck out across the Maiden's Bridge and up along the stream. The snow crunched under his heavy boots, and his feet were frightfully cold. Once more the wind began to howl, and great lumps of snow fell from the trees; the messenger caught a full load of it on his head and under his scarf; a trickle of icy water ran down his back. But what plagued him most was that his feet were slipping wickedly on the hardened snow, and his path now ran steeply up the slope. Next moment he was caught in a hurricane of snow. Like a white wall it came crashing down upon him. Before the messenger had a chance to turn, he got the full force of it in his face; he bent forward with the utmost effort, gasping for breath. He took a step upward and fell. Then he sat up with his back to the wind, but he was seized with a dread of being buried by the snow. He got up and tried to scramble on, but slipped again, fell on both hands, pulled himself up again, but slid backward a good way. He held on to the trees to steady himself, breathing heavily. "Curse it," he said to himself, "I've got to get up there somehow."

He managed to take a few steps, but fell once more, and slid downwards on his stomach. He began to crawl on all fours. His gloves were wet, the snow was inside his leggings, but he must push on. Anything rather than stay there! Melting snow and sweat poured down his cheeks. He could not see for the driving snow, and it looked as though he had lost his way; it made him weep aloud as he crept toilsomely upward. But it was hard work crawling along on all fours in a long coat; he stood up again and stepped forward, battling with the blizzard. For every half-step he made forward he slipped two steps back; he did climb a little farther, but then his feet flew out from under him, and he slid downward with his face buried in the prickly snow. When he picked himself up, he found that he had lost his stick.

Meanwhile clouds of snow were flying over the mountains, massing on the rocks, hissing, bellowing, roaring. The messenger sobbed aloud, gasping with terror and exertion; he climbed on, stopped, took another step and another, halted, turned his back to the wind and took a deep breath through his burning mouth, and then—O Christ in Heaven!—took one step more. He held on to a tree. What was the time? With the greatest effort he drew out his turnip watch in its transparent yellow case. It was encrusted with snow. Perhaps darkness was

coming on. Should he turn back? But he couldn't
have far to go now!

The fitful gale had changed into a steady blizzard.
Clouds rolled along the slope, a dark and dirty mist
full of hurtling sleet. The snow rushed down hori-
zontally, straight into his face, blocking up the eyes,
nose and mouth; with wet frozen fingers it had to be
dug, half melted, from the cavities of the ears and
eyes. The front of the messenger's body was
covered with a layer of snow two inches thick; his
coat was rigid, as stiff and heavy as a board—you
could not bend it; the cakes of snow on his boot-soles
grew bigger and heavier with every step. And in
the forest it was getting dark. And yet, good
heavens, it was barely two in the afternoon!

Suddenly a greenish-yellow darkness poured over
the forest, and the snow gushed down like a cloud-
burst. Flakes the size of your hand, wet and heavy,
flew whirling by so thickly that the dividing line
between earth and air was lost. A man cannot see
a step in front of him. He breathes the flakes in,
wades on through the roaring blizzard that dashes
high over his head, pushes on blindly as if he were
cutting a little passage down there under the snow.
He has but one overmastering instinct—to push on.
He yearns for one thing only—to breathe something
other than snow. He can no longer lift his feet from
the snow; he drags them through the drifts reaching

half-way to his hips; he makes a track which instantly closes up behind him.

Meanwhile in the cities far below a few sparse flakes fluttered down to be melted into black mud. The lights were lit in the shops, the cafés were all aglow, people sat around under the electric globes and grumbled what a miserable gloomy day it was. Numberless lights were ablaze all over the great city, sparkling in the watery mire.

One solitary glimmer shone over the storm-swept field on the mountain. It pierced with difficulty through the falling snow, wavered up and down, and nearly expired; nevertheless, it was there, still shining. There was a light in the Hut in Bear Valley.

It was five o'clock, and therefore pitch-dark, when a shapeless something stopped in front of the Hut in Bear Valley. That "something" spread out its thick white wings and began to beat its body with them and peel off a coating of snow four inches thick. Beneath the snow a coat became visible, and below the coat two feet, and these feet stamped on the stone door-step, till great lumps of snow dropped from them. It was the messenger from Spindelmühl.

He entered the hut and saw a thin gentleman sitting at the table. He tried to utter a greeting, but his voice failed him completely. It only made a little wheezing noise like that of escaping steam.

The other man rose: "My good man, what the devil brings you here in a blizzard like this? Why, you might never have got through alive!"

The messenger nodded and gurgled.

"If it isn't absolute madness!" growled the other, and told the servant to bring some tea. "Well, where were you making for, then, dad? Martin's Hut?"

The messenger shook his head and opened his leather pouch; it was full of snow; he took out a telegram frozen so stiff that it crackled.

"Bha, bha, Bharek?" he croaked out hoarsely.

"What do you say?" asked the other.

"Is . . . anyone . . . here . . . named . . . Mar . . . ek, an . . . Eng . . . i . . . neer?" the messenger stammered out with a reproachful look.

"That's me," the thin gentlemen cried. "Have you something for me? Let me see it, quick!"

Marek tore open the telegram. It read:

"Your predictions confirmed. BONDY."

Nothing more.

CHAPTER XXII

THE OLD PATRIOT

I N the Prague office of the *People's Journal* everyone was working at top speed. The telephone
operator was yelling furiously into the telephone
and quarrelling with the young lady at the Exchange.
Scissors clicked and typewriters clattered, and Mr.
Cyril Keval sat on the table and dangled his legs.

"I say, they're holding a meeting at Vaclavak,"
he said in a low voice. "Some Communist's up there
preaching voluntary poverty. He's haranguing the
people, telling them they ought to be like the lilies
of the field. He's got a beard right down to his
waist. What a frightful lot of long-bearded chaps
there are about nowadays! All looking like
apostles."

"Mhm," answered old Rejzek, turning over the
papers from the Czechoslovak Press Bureau.

"What makes their beards grow so long?" Mr.
Keval ruminated. "I say, Rejzek, I do believe the
Absolute has something to do with that as well.
Golly, Rejzek, I'm afraid of something of the sort
growing on me. Just imagine it, right down to the
waist!"

"Mhm," Mr. Rejzek said ponderously.

"The Free Thought Society is holding a service in Havliček Square to-day. Father Novaček is performing miracles in Tyl Square. There's sure to be a row between them, you'll see. Yesterday Novaček healed a man who had been lame from birth. Then they had a procession, and just think, the fellow who'd been lame gave a Jew an awful hiding. Broke three of his ribs or more. He was a Zionist, see."

"Mhm," remarked Mr. Rejzek, marking some items of news.

"There's *certain* to be a dust-up to-day, Rejzek," Keval expatiated. "The Progressives are holding a meeting in the Old Town Square. They've trotted out 'Away from Rome' again. And Father Novaček is organizing the Maccabeans; you know, a sort of Catholic armed guard. You wait, there will be a scrimmage. The Archbishop has forbidden Novaček to perform miracles, but his Reverence is like one possessed; he even goes and raises the dead."

"Mhm," said Mr. Rejzek, and went on marking copy.

"I had a letter from my mother," Cyril Keval confided in subdued tones. "At home in Moravia, you know, near Hustopec and thereabouts, they're simply raving mad with the Czechs—say they're heathen and heretics and idolaters and want to set up new gods, and all that stuff. They've shot a gamekeeper there because he was a Czech. I tell you, Rejzek, things are fairly seething everywhere."

"Mhm," came Mr. Rejzek's sign of acquiescence.

"They've even gone for each other in the synagogue," continued Mr. Keval. "The Zionists gave the people who believe in Baal a fearful licking. There were even three people killed. And have you heard about the split among the Communists? There you are, I nearly forgot about it; that's another grand mix-up. Now we're going to have the mystic Communists, a sort of left wing; then the Christians, Marians, Scientists, Resurrectionites, textile Knights of St. John, iron Knights, miner Knights, and about seven other parties. Now they're squabbling about the sick benefit funds and the workmen's dwellings. Just wait, I'm going to slip over to Hybernska Street this afternoon. My boy, the garrison was confined to barracks this afternoon; but in the meantime the Vršovice barracks have sent an ultimatum to the Černin barracks calling on them to recognize the Vršovice dogma of the Three Degrees of Salvation. If they don't accept the doctrine, they are to report for battle at Sandberk. The Dejvice artillerymen have gone to the Černin barracks to disband. The Vršovice garrison has barricaded itself in, the soldiers have planted machine-guns in the windows and declared war. They are being besieged by the Seventh Dragoons, the Castle Guard, and four light batteries. They've been given six hours, then the firing will begin. Rejzek, it's a real pleasure to be alive in these days."

"Mhm," said Mr. Rejzek.

"Yes, and at the University to-day," Keval went on quietly, "the natural science faculty and the history faculty came to blows. You know, the natural science faculty, being rather pantheistic, so to speak, disputes the Revelation. The professors conducted the fight, and Deal Radl himself carried the flag. The historians fortified the University Library in the Klementinum and defended themselves desperately, armed with books. Dean Radl got hit on the head with a bound volume of Velenovsky and was killed on the spot. Probably concussion of the brain. The Rector, Arne Novak, was seriously injured by a volume of *Invention and Progress.* Finally the historians buried the attacking party under the Collected Works of Jan Vrba. Now the sappers are at work on the scene of the battle, and so far they've recovered seven corpses, among them three lecturers. I don't think there were more than thirty buried though."

"Mhm," observed Mr. Rejzek.

"Then there's the Sparta Club, my boy," Keval rattled on with mild enthusiasm. "The Sparta has proclaimed that the only God is the Greek Zeus, whereas the Slavia votes for Svantovit, the old sun-god. On Sunday there's to be a match between the two Gods on the Letna. Besides their footballs, both clubs will bring hand-grenades, and the Slavia will also have machine-guns and the Sparta a twelve-centimetre gun. There's a terrific rush for tickets. The supporters of both clubs will be armed. Rejzek, believe me, there will be a shindy! I bet Zeus will win."

"Mhm," said Mr. Rejzek, "but now you might have a look at the post."

"Well, I don't care," cried Cyril Keval. "A man can get used even to a God, can't he? What's the latest from the Press Bureau?"

"Nothing special," growled Mr. Rejzek. "Blood-shed at demonstrations in Rome. They're going for each other in Ulster—you know, the Irish Catholics. The St. Kilda agreement is being repudiated all round. Pogroms in Budapest; a schism in France—the Waldenses have bobbed up there again, and the Anabaptists in Münster. At Bologna an Anti-Pope has been elected, one Father Martin of the Barefoot Friars. And so on. Nothing of local interest. Have a look at the letters, will you."

Cyril Keval stopped talking and began opening the letters. There were a few hundred of them, but he had hardly read half a dozen when he was off once more.

"Look here, Rejzek," he began, "it's the same

tale all the way through. Take this one for instance: From Chrudim. Dear Sir,—As an old subscriber to your esteemed journal, your readers and the whole of the public who are now being harassed by unprofitable disputes"—("He's left out 'will be interested,'" interpolated Mr. Keval)—" 'in the remarkable miracle performed by our local pastor, the Rev. Father Zakoupil.' And so on. In Jicin it was the storekeeper of the Co-operative Society, and in Benesov it was the superintendent of schools. In Chotěbor it was even the widow Jirák, who keeps a tobacco shop. Have I to read all this stuff?"

Work went on again in silence for a while.

"Damn it, Rejzek," Keval burst out again, "I say, do you know what would be a real sensation? A giant gooseberry? A lovely canard? Why, if something were to happen quite in the natural way, without any miracle about it. But I don't think anyone would believe us. Wait a bit, I'll try to think up something natural."

Again there was a brief period of quiet.

"Rejzek," cried Keval mournfully, "I simply can't think up anything natural. When I think it over, everything is a miracle really. Whatever is, is a sort of magic."

Just then the editor-in-chief entered.

"Who did the cuttings from the *Tribune?* Here's a story in it that we haven't got."

"What sort of a story," asked Mr. Rejzek.

"In the Finance and Commerce Section. An American combine has bought up the Pacific Islands and is subletting them. A tiny coral atoll costs fifty thousand dollars a year. Big demand even from the Continent of Europe. Shares have gone up to two thousand seven hundred already. G. H. Bondy interested to the extent of one hundred and twenty millions. And we haven't got a word about it," said the editor-in-chief angrily, and slammed the door behind him.

"Rejzek," cried Keval, "here's an interesting letter: 'Dear Sir,—Forgive an old patriot, who can remember the evil times of oppression and the dark days of serfdom, if he raises a plaintive voice and begs you to use your skilful pen to make known to the Czech people the grief and sore anxiety we old patriots feel . . .' and so on. Farther on he says: 'In our ancient and glorious nation we see brother egged on against brother; innumerable parties, sects, and churches struggling together like wolves and destroying each other in their mutual hatred'—(must be some very old chap; his writing is terribly shaky) —'while our ancient enemy prowls around us like a roaring lion, filling the minds of our people with the German watchword of "Away from Rome," and supported by those mistaken patriots who set the interests of their party before the national unity for

which we yearn. And we behold with anguish and
sorrow the prospect of a new battle of Lipany, where
Czech ranged against Czech under the cloak of
different religious watchwords, will be left lying on
the bloody field. And so, alas, the words of the
Scriptures about a kingdom divided against itself
will be fulfilled. And there shall be piercing and
felling of many, as it is written in our own glorious
and authentic cycles of chivalry.' "

"That's enough," said Mr. Rejzek.

"Wait a bit; here he talks about the hypertrophy
of parties and churches. It is a hereditary Czech
disease, he says. 'Of this there cannot be the slightest doubt, as Dr. Kramář used to say. And therefore, I solemnly adjure you at this twelfth hour,
when great and terrible dangers confront us on
every hand, to urge our people to band themselves
together in a union of the whole nation for the
defence of our country. If a religious bond be
necessary for this union, then let us be neither
Protestants nor Catholics nor Monists nor Ab-
stainers, but let us adopt a single, Slav, powerful, and
brotherly Orthodox faith, which will unite us in
one great Slav family and will secure for us in these
stormy times the protection of a powerful Slav ruler.
Those who will not freely and whole-heartedly pay
allegiance to this glorious pan-Slav ideal should be
forced by Government authority, yea, and by every

form of compulsion permissible in these exceptional circumstances, to abandon their partisan and sectarian interests in favour of the union of the whole nation.' And so on. Signed 'An Old Patriot.' What do you say to that?"

"Nothing," said Mr. Rejzek.

"I think that there's something in it," Mr. Keval began; but just then the telephone operator entered and said, "Munich on the 'phone. Some sort of civil or religious war broke out in Germany yesterday. Is it worth putting in the paper?"

CHAPTER XXIII

THE AUGSBURG IMBROGLIC

By 11 p. m. the following telephonic communications had been received at the office of the *People's Journal:*—

CZECH PRESS BUREAU. *From Munich,* 12th inst.— According to the Wolff Telegraph Agency, the demonstrations in Augsburg yesterday led to bloodshed. Seventy Protestants were killed. The demonstrations are still in progress.

CZECH PRESS BUREAU. *From Berlin,* 12th inst.—It is officially announced that the number of killed and wounded at Augsburg does not exceed twelve. The police are maintaining order.

SPECIAL MESSAGE. *From Lugano,* 12th inst.—We learn from a reliable source that the number of victims at Augsburg is over five thousand. Railway communication with the north is suspended. The Bavarian Ministry is in permanent session. The German Emperor has broken off his hunting trip and is returning to Berlin.

CZECH PRESS BUREAU. *Reuter,* 12th inst.—At 3 a. m. to-day the Bavarian Government declared a Holy War on Prussia.

By the following day Mr. Cyril Keval was already in Bavaria. From his comparatively trustworthy reports we make the following excerpts:—

At 6 p.m. on the 10th instant the Catholic workmen in the Scholler lead-pencil factory at Augsburg gave the Protestant foreman a beating, the provocation being some dispute relating to the worship of the Virgin. Quiet prevailed at night, but at 10 a.m. on the following day the Catholic workmen came out in all departments noisily demanding the discharge of all Protestant employees. Scholler, the owner of the factory, was killed, and two directors were stabbed. The clergy were compelled by force to carry the monstrance at the head of the procession. The Archbishop, Dr. Lenz, who came out to pacify the demonstrators, was thrown into the River Lech. The Social-Democratic leaders attempted to speak, but were forced to take refuge in the synagogue. At 3 p.m. the synagogue was blown up with dynamite. While the looting of Jewish and Protestant shops went on, accompanied by some shooting and numerous conflagrations, the City Council carried unanimously the Immaculate Conception of the Virgin Mary, and issued an impassioned appeal to the Catholic nations of the world to take up the sword in defence of the Holy Catholic Faith. Upon the receipt of this news various manifestos were issued in other Bavarian cities. In Munich a Popular Assembly was held at 7 p.m., which amid the wildest enthusiasm passed a resolution for the secession of the Southern States from the German Empire. The Munich Government wired Berlin that it was taking over the administration. The Imperial Chancellor, Dr. Wurm, immediately called on the Minister of War, who ordered ten thousand bayonets to Bavaria from the garrisons of Saxony and the Rhineland. At 1 a.m. these troop trains were blown up on the line at the Bavarian frontier, and machine guns were turned upon the wounded. At 3 a.m. the Munich Government, in alliance with the Alpine provinces, decided to proclaim a Holy War on the Lutherans.

It would seem that hopes of a peaceful solution of the whole misunderstanding have not yet been abandoned in

Berlin. At this moment the Emperor is still delivering his speech in Parliament, declaring that he knows neither Catholics nor Protestants, but only Germans. The North German forces are said to be concentrated along the Erfurt-Gotha-Kassel line. The Catholic forces are advancing in the general direction of Zwickau and Rudolfstadt, meeting with no opposition but that of the civilian population. The town of Greiz has been burned down and the citizens either killed or dragged into slavery. The reports of a great battle have not so far been confirmed. Refugees from Bayreuth state that the firing of heavy artillery could be heard from the north. The railway station at Madgeburg is said to have been blown up by the bombs of Bavarian airmen. Weimar is on fire.

Indescribable enthusiasm prevails here in Munich. Attestation commissions are at work in all the schools; crowds of volunteers wait as long as twenty hours in the streets. The heads of twenty decapitated pastors are exposed on the Rathaus. The Catholic clergy have to serve mass day and night in overcrowded churches; the Reverend Father Grosshube, who was also a member of Parliament, died of exhaustion at the altar. Jews, Monists, Abstinents, and other heretics have barricaded themselves in their houses. Rosenheim, the banker, the oldest member of the Jewish community, was publicly burned at the stake this morning.

The Dutch and Danish ambassadors have asked for their passports. The American representative has lodged a protest against the disturbance of the peace; on the other hand, the Italian Government has assured Bavaria of its particularly benevolent neutrality.

Bands of recruits march through the streets carrying flags with a white cross on a red ground, and shouting "God wills it." Ladies are entering the nursing service and getting hospitals ready. Business houses are for the most part closed. So is the Stock Exchange.

That was on the 14th of February. On the 15th fairly heavy fighting took place on both banks of the Werre, the Protestant forces yielding a little ground. On the same day the first shots were also fired on the Dutch-Belgian frontier. England ordered the mobilization of the fleet.

On the 16th of February Italy granted free passage to the Spanish army despatched to the aid of the Bavarians. The Tyrolese peasants, armed with scythes, attacked the Helvetian Swiss.

On the 18th of February, the Anti-Pope Martin cabled his blessing to the Bavarian army. An indecisive battle took place at Meiningen. Russia declared war on the Polish Catholics.

February 19th: Ireland declared war on England. An opposition Caliph made his appearance at Broussa, and unfurled the green banner of the Prophet. Mobilization of the Balkan States, and massacres in Macedonia.

February 23rd: The North German front pierced. General revolt in India. Proclamation of a Holy War by the Moslems on the Christians.

February 27th: The Greek-Italian war, and the first encounters on Albanian soil.

March 3rd: The Japanese fleet sailed eastward against the United States of America.

March 15th: The Crusaders (Catholics) took Berlin. Meanwhile the Union of Protestant States was proclaimed at Stettin. The German Emperor, Kaspar I, assumed command in person.

March 16th: A Chinese army, two million strong, poured over the Siberian and Manchurian frontiers. The army of the Anti-Pope Martin took Rome by storm. Pope Urban fled to Portugal.

March 18th: Spain demanded that the Lisbon Government should deliver up Pope Urban; refusal followed *ipso facto* by war between Spain and Portugal.

March 26th: The South American States presented an ultimatum to the North American Union, demanding the repeal of Prohibition and the abolition of religious liberty.

March 27th: The Japanese fleet landed troops in California and British Columbia.

On April 1st the world situation was approximately as follows: In Central Europe the great world-conflict between the Catholics and Protestants was running its course. The Protestant Union had forced back the Crusaders out of Berlin, had got a firm hold on Saxony, and had occupied even the neutral territory of Czechoslovakia. The City of Prague was, by a peculiar coincidence, under the command of the Swedish Major-General Wrangel, possibly a descendant of the general of the same name who figured in the Thirty Years' War. On

the other hand, the Crusaders had made themselves
masters of Holland, which they had flooded by
breaking the dykes and letting in the sea, as well as
of Hanover and Holstein as far as Lübeck, whence
they were making inroads on Denmark. No quarter
was given in the fighting. Cities were razed to the
ground, the men killed, and women up to the age of
fifty violated. But the first things destroyed in
every case were the enemy Karburators. Contem-
poraries of these inordinately bloody struggles
assure us that supernatural powers were fighting on
both sides. Often it seemed as though an invisible
hand seized hostile aircraft and dashed them to the
ground, or intercepted in its flight a fifty-four centi-
metre projectile weighing a ton and hurled it back
upon its own ranks. Particularly horrible were the
scenes enacted during the destruction of the Karburators. As soon as the enemy position was
occupied, there ensued an invisible but desperate
struggle round the local Karburators. At times it
was like a cyclone which wrecked and scattered the
whole building in which an atomic boiler stood, like
someone blowing on a heap of feathers. Bricks,
timbers and tiles flew round in wild confusion, and
the contest usually ended in a frightful explosion
which felled every tree and structure within a radius
of twelve kilometres and scooped out a crater over
two hundred metres deep. The force of the detona-

tion naturally varied according to the size of the exploding Karburator.

Suffocating gases spread over a radius of three hundred kilometres, utterly blasting all vegetation; however, as these creeping clouds several times turned back upon their own ranks—through the strategical intervention of supernatural powers—this very unreliable method of warfare was abandoned. It was apparent that while the Absolute attacked on one side, it also defended itself on the other. It introduced unheard-of weapons into warfare—earthquakes, cyclones, showers of sulphur, inundations, angels, pestilence, famines, plagues of locusts, etc.—till there was no alternative but to alter the art of military stategy altogether. Mass attacks, permanent entrenchments, open order, strong points, and such-like nonsense, were abandoned; every soldier received a knife, some cartridges, and some bombs, and with these he went off on his own to kill any soldier who wore on his breast a cross of a different colour. It was not a matter of two armies confronting each other. There was simply a particular country which was the battlefield, and there the two armies moved about promiscuously, killing one another off, man for man, until finally it became clear to whom that country now belonged. It was a terribly murderous method, to be sure, but it had ultimately, in the long run, a certain conclusiveness.

Such was the situation in Central Europe. At the beginning of April the Protestant armies were entering Austria and Bavaria by way of Czechoslovakia, while the Catholics were overrunning Denmark and Pomerania. Holland, as already stated, had completely vanished from the map of Europe.

In Italy internal warfare was raging between the parties of Urban and Martin: meanwhile Sicily fell into the hands of the Greek Evzones. The Portuguese occupied Austria and Castile, but lost their own Estramadura; in the South as a whole the war was waged with quite exceptional ferocity.

England had been fighting on Irish soil and then in the colonies. By the beginning of April she held only the coastline of Egypt. The other colonies had been lost, and the settlers killed by the natives. With the aid of the Arabians, Sudanese, and Persian armies the Turks had overwhelmed the entire Balkan region, and had made themselves masters of Hungary, when the schism broke out between the Shiahs and the Sunnis on what was apparently a very important question concerning Ali, the fourth Caliph. Both sects pursued each other from Constantinople to the Carpathians with a zeal and bloodthirstiness which unfortunately also vented itself upon the

Christians. And so in this part of Europe things were worse than anywhere else.

Poland vanished, being wiped out of existence by the Russian armies. The Russian hosts then turned to face the Yellow invasion which was sweeping northward and westward. Meanwhile ten Japanese army corps had been landed in North America.

You will notice that no mention has yet been made of France, the chronicler having reserved that country for Chapter XXIV.

CHAPTER XXIV

THE NAPOLEON OF THE MOUNTAIN BRIGADE

BOBINET, if you please, Toni Bobinet, the twenty-two-year-old lieutenant of mountain artillery, attached to the garrison of Annecy (Haute Savoie), but at present on six weeks' manœuvres on the Needles (Les Aiguilles), from which on a clear day one can see in the west the lakes of Annecy and Geneva, and in the east the blunted ridge of the Bonne Montagne and the peaks of Mont Blanc— do you know your way about now? Well, then, Lieutenant Toni Bobinet sat on a boulder and tugged at his tiny moustache, first because he was bored, and secondly because he had read a newspaper two weeks old right through for the fifth time, and was now thinking things over.

At this point the chronicler ought to follow the meditations of the prospective Napoleon, but in the meantime his glance (the chronicler's, that is) had slid along the snow-covered slopes to the gorge of the Arly, where the thaw had already set in, and where his eye is caught and held by the tiny little towns of Mégève, Flumet, and Ugines, with their pointed churches looking like toys. Ah, the memories of long-vanished childhood! The castles in the air one reared with one's box of bricks!

Meanwhile Lieutenant Bobinet . . . but no. Let us abandon any attempt to psychologize great men, to express the titanic idea in the germ from which it sprang. We are not equal to the task, and if we were, we should perhaps be disappointed. Just picture to yourself this little Lieutenant Bobinet sitting on Les Aiguilles with Europe falling into ruin all about him—a battery of mountain guns in front of him, and below him a miniature world which could easily be shot to pieces from where he sat. Imagine that he has just read in an old copy of the Annecy *Moniteur* the leading article in which some M. Babillard calls for the strong hand of a helmsman who will steer the good ship France out of the raging storm toward new power and glory; and that up there, at a height of over two thousand metres, the air is pure and free from the Absolute, so that one can think clearly and freely. Picture all this, and you will understand how it was that Lieutenant Bobinet, sitting there on his rock, first grew very thoughtful and then wrote his venerable, wrinkled, white-haired mother a somewhat confused letter, assuring her that "she would soon be hearing of her Toni," and that Toni had "a magnificent idea." After that he saw to one thing and another, had a

good night's sleep, and in the morning assembled all
the soldiers of his battery, deposed the incompetent
old captain, took possession of the military post at
Sallanches, declared war on the Absolute with
Napoleonic brevity, and went to sleep again. The
following day he shot to pieces the Karburator in the
bakery at Thônes, occupied the railway station of
Bonneville, and seized the command at Annecy, having by this time three thousand men under him.
Within a week he had destroyed over two hundred
Karburators and was leading fifteen thousand
bayonets and sabres against Grenoble. He was proclaimed commandant of Grenoble, and now had a
small army of forty thousand men at his back, with
which he descended into the valley of the Rhone and
busied himself in painstakingly clearing the sur-
rounding territory of all atomic motors by means of
his long-range guns. On the road to Chambéry he
captured the Minister for War, who was hurrying in
his motor-car to put Bobinet back in his place. The
Minister for War was so captivated and convinced
by Bobinet's plans that he made him a General on
the following day. On April 1st the city of Lyons
was completely cleansed of every trace of the
Absolute.

Up to this point Bobinet's triumphant progress
had not been attended by bloodshed. He met with
his first opposition from ardent Catholics beyond

the Loire, and sanguinary engagements took place. Fortunately for Bobinet, many Frenchmen had remained sceptics, even in communities completely saturated with the Absolute, and indeed showed themselves wildly fanatical in their unbelief and rationalism. After cruel massacres and new St. Bartholomew's Eves "les Bobinets" were welcomed everywhere as liberators, and everywhere they went they succeeded in pacifying the populace after destroying all the Karburators.

And so it befell that as early as July, Parliament proclaimed that Toni Bobinet had deserved well of his country and raised him to the dignity of First Consul with the title of Marshal. France was consolidated. Bobinet introduced State atheism; any sort of religious demonstration was punishable by court-martial with death.

We cannot refrain from mentioning a few episodes in the great man's career.

BOBINET AND HIS MOTHER.—One day Bobinet was holding council at Versailles with his General Staff. As the day was hot, he had taken his place by an open window. Suddenly he noticed an aged woman in the park, warming herself in the sun. Bobinet at once interrupted Marshal Jollivet with a cry of "Look, gentlemen . . . my mother!" All present, even the most hardened generals, were moved to tears by this demonstration of filial affection.

BOBINET AND LOVE OF COUNTRY.—On one occasion Bobinet was holding a military review on the Champ de Mars in a downpour of rain. While the heavy howitzers were passing before him, an army motor ran into a large puddle of water which spurted up and bespattered Bobinet's cloak. Marshal Jollivet wished to punish the commander of the unfortunate battery by reducing him in rank on the spot. But Bobinet restrained him, saying, "Let him alone, Marshal. After all, this is the mud of France!"

BOBINET AND THE OLD PENSIONER.—Bobinet was once driving out incognito to Chartres. On the way a tyre burst, and while the chauffeur was putting on a new one, a one-legged pensioner came up and asked for alms.

"Where did this man lose his leg?" asked Bobinet.

The old pensioner related that he had lost it while serving in Indo-China. He had a poor old mother, and there were often days when neither of them had a bite to eat.

"Marshal, take this man's name," said Bobinet, deeply affected. And sure enough a week later there came a knock at the door of the old pensioner's hut;

it was Bobinet's personal courier, who handed the
hapless cripple a packet "from the First Consul."
Who can describe the surprise and delight of the
old soldier when upon opening the packet he found
inside it *the Bronze Medal!*

Thanks to a character of such striking qualities,
it is not surprising that Bobinet finally consented to
gratify the fervent desire of the whole nation, and
on the 14th of August proclaimed himself, amid
universal enthusiasm, Emperor of the French.

The whole world thus entered upon a period
which, though anything but peaceful, was to be
glorious in history.   Every quarter of the globe
literally blazed with heroic feats of arms. Seen from
Mars, our earth must certainly have shone like a
star of the first magnitude, from which the Martian
astronomers doubtless concluded that we were still
in a condition of glowing heat.   You can well believe
that chivalrous France and her representative, the
Emperor Toni Bobinet, did not play a minor rôle.
Perhaps, too, such remnants of the Absolute as had
not yet escaped into space were at work here, awak-
ening a spirit of exaltation and fervour.   At any
rate, when the great Emperor proclaimed, two days
after his coronation, that the hour had come for
France to cover the whole earth with her banner, a
unanimous roar of enthusiasm gave him his answer.

Bobinet's plan was the following:—

1. To occupy Spain, and by taking Gibraltar secure the key to the Mediterranean Sea.

2. To occupy the Danube valley as far as Budapest as the key to the interior of Europe.

3. To occupy Denmark as the key to the North Sea area.

And since territorial keys have usually to be smeared with blood, France fitted out three armies which won for her tremendous glory.

The fourth army occupied Asia Minor as the key to the East.

The fifth army made itself master of the mouth of the St. Lawrence as the key to America.

The sixth army went down in the naval battle off the English coast.

The seventh army laid seige to Sebastopol.

By New Year's Eve, 1944, the Emperor Bobinet had all his keys in the pocket of his artillery breeches.

CHAPTER XXV

THE SO-CALLED GREATEST WAR

IT is a foible of our human nature that when we have an extremely unpleasant experience, it gives up a peculiar satisfaction if it is "the biggest" of its disagreeable kind that has happened since the world began. During a heat wave, for instance, we are very pleased if the papers announce that it is "the highest temperature reached since the year 1881," and we feel a little resentment towards the year 1881 for having gone us one better. Or if our ears are frozen till all the skin peels off, it fills us with a certain happiness to learn that "it was the hardest frost recorded since 1786." It is just the same with wars. The war in progress is either the most righteous or the bloodiest, or the most successful, or the longest, since such and such a time; any superlative whatever always affords us the proud satisfaction of having been through something extraordinary and record-breaking.

Well, the war which lasted from February 12, 1944, to the autumn of 1953, was in all truthfulness and without exaggeration (on my honour!) the Greatest War. Do not let us rob those who lived through it of this one solitary and well-earned satisfaction. 198,000,000 men took part in the fighting, and all but thirteen of them fell. I could give you figures by which accountants and statisticians have attempted to illustrate these enormous losses—for instance, how many thousand kilometres the bodies would stretch if laid one beside the other, and for how many hours an express train would have to run if the bodies were put on the line in place of sleepers; or if the index fingers of all the fallen were cut off and put in sardine-tins, how many hundred goods trucks could be filled with such a load, and so on. But I have a poor memory for figures, and I don't want to cheat you out of a single miserable statistical truck-load. So I repeat that it was the greatest war since the creation of the world, whether you take into consideration the loss of life or the extent of the theatre of war.

Once again the present chronicler has to excuse himself for not caring very much for descriptions of events on the grand scale. Perhaps he ought to relate how the war swung from the Rhine to the Euphrates, from Korea to Denmark, from Lugano to Haparanda, and so forth. Instead of this, he would far rather depict the arrival of the Bedouins in their white burnouses at Geneva, and how they came galloping in with the heads of their enemies stuck on their six-foot spears; or the love

adventures of a French *poilu* in Thibet; the caval-
cades of Russian Cossacks that crossed the Sahara;
the nightly encounters of Macedonia *comitadjis* with
Senegalese sharpshooters on the shores of the lakes
of Finland. As you see, there is the greatest diver-
sity of material. Bobinet's victorious regiments flew,
so to speak, in one dazzling swoop in the footprints
of Alexander the Great across India to China; but
meanwhile the Yellow invasion swept over Siberia
and Russia into France and Spain, thus cutting off
from their native land the Moslems who were
operating in Sweden. The Russian regiments,
retreating before the overwhelming numerical supe-
riority of the Chinese, found themselves in North
Africa, where Sergei Nikolayevich Zlocin established
his Czardom. He was soon murdered, however,
because his Bavarian generals conspired against his
Prussian hetmans, and Sergei Fyodorovich Zlosin
thereupon ascended the Imperial throne in Tim-
buctoo.

Czechoslovakia was held by the Swedes, French,
Turks, Russians and Chinese in succession; each of
these invasions killed off the native population to
the last man. In the course of those years services
were held, or Mass celebrated, in the Church of St.
Vitus by a pastor, a solicitor, an Imam, an Archimandrite and a bonze, none of them enjoying any
permanent success. The only gratifying change was

that the Stavovsky Theatre was invariably full, being used for the purposes of an army store.

When the Japanese had thrust the Chinese out of Eastern Europe in the year 1951 there arose for a brief space a new Middle Kingdom (as the Chinese call their native land), and chance willed that it should fall precisely within the frontier of the old empire of Austria-Hungary. Once again an aged ruler dwelt in Schönbrunn, the old mandarin Jaja Wir Weana, one hundred and six years old, "to whose consecrated head rejoicing nations turn their eyes with child-like love," as the *Wiener Mittagszeitung* assured its readers daily. The official language was Chinese, which at one sweep did away with all nationalistic rivalries. The State god was Buddha. The stubborn Catholics of Bohemia and Moravia moved out of the country, or became the victims of Chinese dragonades and confiscations, by which the number of national martyrs was increased to a remarkable extent. On the other hand, several prominent and prudent Czech patriots were exalted to mandarin rank by Most Gracious Decree as a reward for their enlightened adaptability. The Chinese administration inaugurated many new and progressive measures, such as the issuing of tickets in place of provisions; but the Middle Kingdom fell to pieces very early, as the supply of lead necessary for munitions ran out, and all authority thereupon collapsed. A few of those Chinese who were not killed remained in the country even in the ensuing period of peace, and for the most part occupied high Government positions.

In the meantime the Emperor Bobinet, now residing in India, at Simla, learnt that an Amazon Empire of women existed in the hitherto unexplored river-territory of the Irawaddy, Salwin, and Mekong. He set out for that region at once with his Old Guard, but never again returned. According to one version he married and settled there. According to another, Amalia, the Queen of the Amazons, cut off his head in battle and flung it into a skin filled with blood, saying, "Satia te sanguine, quem tantum sitisti." This second verson is doubtless the milder.

In the end Europe became the theatre of furious struggles between the black race, which came pouring out of the interior of Africa, and the Mongolian race. The happenings of those two years are best passed over in silence. The last traces of civilization vanished. . For instance, the bears multiplied on Hradcany to such an extent that the last inhabitants of Prague destroyed all the bridges, even the Charles Bridge, to save the right bank of the Vltava from these bloodthirsty beasts. The population shrank to an insignificant little group; the Vyšehrad Chapter died out both on the male and female side; the championship match between the Sparta Club and the Victoria Zizkov was witnessed by only one hundred and ten people.

On the other continents the situation was no better. North America, after the fearful ravages of the murderous struggles between the Prohibitionists and the "Wets," had become a Japanese colony. In South America there had been by turns an Empire of Uruguay, Chili, Peru, Brandenburg and Patagonia. In Australia, an Ideal State had been formed, immediately after the downfall of England, which transformed this promising land into an uninhabited desert. In Africa over two million white men had been eaten. The negroes of the Congo basin had hurled themselves upon Europe, while the rest of Africa was in the throes of the fluctuating conflicts of its one hundred and eighty-six different Emperors, Sultans, Kings, Chiefs and Presidents.

Such is history, you see. Each one of those hundred millions of warring pigmies had had his childhood, his loves, his plans; he was often afraid, he was frequently a hero, but usually he was tired to death and would have been glad to lie down on his bed in peace; and if he died, it was certainly against his will. And from all of this, one can take only a handful of arid events: a battle here or there, losses so and so, result this or that—and, after all, the result never brought about any real decision.

Therefore I say: Do not rob the people of that

time of their only boast—that what they went through was the Greatest War. We, however, know that in a few decades we shall succeed in arranging an even greater war, for in this respect also the human race is progressing ever upward and on.

CHAPTER XXVI

THE present chronicler now appeals to August Sedlaček, Joseph Pekař, and other authorities on the writing of history, in support of the statement that a vast amount of historical knowledge can be drawn from purely local happenings. They mirror world events as in a drop of water.

Well, then, the drop of water entitled Hradec Králové is memorable to the chronicler because he used to race about in it like a tiny organism, as an infusorian of the grammar school there, and not surprisingly thought it the universe; but enough of that.

The Greatest War found Hradec Králové armed with only a single Karburator, and that was in the brewery still standing to this day behind the Church of the Holy Spirit, which is next to the residence of the Canons. Perhaps it was this hallowed environment which reacted on the Absolute in such a way that it began to brew a plentiful and ardently Catholic beer and thereby brought the citizens of Hradec to a condition in which the deceased Bishop Brynch would have taken sincere pleasure.

However, Hradec Králové is too close to the railway, and so it very soon fell into the hands of the Prussians, who in their Lutheran fury destroyed the Karburator in the brewery. Nevertheless, mindful of its historical continuity, Hradec maintained an agreeable religious temperature, especially when the enlightened Bishop Linda took over the diocese. And even when the Bobinets, the Turks, and the Chinese came, Hradec did not lose its proud consciousness that (i) it had the best amateur theatre in all Eastern Bohemia; (ii) it had the tallest steeple in Eastern Bohemia; (iii) the pages of its local history contained the greatest battle in Eastern Bohemia. Heartened by these reflections, Hradec Králové withstood the most terrible trials of the Greatest War.

When the Mandarin Empire collapsed, the city was under the government of that circumspect Burgomaster, Mr. Skocdopole. Amid the prevailing anarchy his administration was blessed with comparative peace, thanks to the wise counsels of Bishop Linda and the Worshipful City Fathers. But one fine day there came to the city a poor tailor, Hampl by name; he was, Heaven help us, a native of Hradec, but he had knocked about the world ever since childhood and had even served with the Foreign Legion in Algeria—in fact, an adventurer. He marched with Bobinet's troops to the conquest of India, but deserted near Baghdad, and had slipped like a needle through the lines of the Bashi-Bazouks, French, Swedes and Chinese, back to his native city.

Well, this Hampl, the little tailor, had caught a whiff of Bobinetism, and as soon as he got back to Hradec he thought of nothing but how he could seize command. Stitching away at clothes didn't suit him any longer, thank you; so he began agitating and criticizing, saying that one thing and another was not right, that the whole City Council was under the thumb of the parsons, and what about that money in the Savings Bank, and Mr. Skocdopole was an incapable old dodderer, and what not. Wars, unfortunately, bring with them a demoralization and a weakening of all authority, and so Hampl found several followers and with their assistance founded the Social-Revolutionary Party.

One day in June friend Hampl summoned a Popular Assembly in the Little Square, and standing on the fountain, shouted out, among other things, that the people categorically demanded that Skocdopole, that scoundrel, reactionary, and lackey of the Bishop, should resign the office of Burgomaster.

In answer to this, Mr. Skocdopole put up posters stating that he, as the lawfully elected Burgomaster, need take orders from no one, least of all from an interloper and a deserter; that in the present times of unrest it was impossible to hold a fresh election, and that our clear-sighted citizens were well aware . . . and so forth. This was just what Hampl was waiting for to carry out his coup *à la Bobinet*. He came out of his house on the Little Square, waving a red flag, with two boys behind him beating drums with all their might. In this fashion he marched around the Great Square, paused a while in front of the Bishop's palace, and then marched off with rolling drums to the field near the Orlice river called the "Little Mill." There he stuck his standard into the ground and, seated on a drum, wrote out his declaration of war. Then he sent the two boys into the city with orders to beat their drums and read out his proclamation at every corner; it ran as follows:

IN THE NAME OF HIS HIGHNESS THE EMPEROR BOBINET, I hereby summon the royal City of Hradec Králové to place the keys of the city gates in my hands. If this is not done by sunset, I will put into effect the military measures I have prepared and will attack the city at dawn with artillery, cavalry and bayonets. I will spare the lives and property only of those who join my camp at the "Little Mill" by dawn at latest, bringing all their usable weapons, and take the oath of allegiance to His Majesty the Emperor Bobinet. Parlementaires will be shot. The Emperor does not parley.
GENERAL HAMPL.

This proclamation was read out and caused a considerable commotion, especially when the sexton of the Church of the Holy Spirit began to ring the

tocsin in the White Tower.   Mr. Skocdopole called
on Bishop Linda, who, however, laughed at his fears.
Then he summoned an extraordinary meeting of the
City Council, at which he proposed that the keys of
the city gates should be given up to General Hampl.
It was then ascertained that there were no such keys
in existence; a few locks and keys of historical
interest which used to repose in the City Museum
had been carried off by the Swedes.   Amid these
perplexities night came on.

All the afternoon, but more particularly towards
evening, people were trickling along the pleasant
lanes towards the Little Mill.   "Oh, well," they
said to each other when they met, "I thought I might
as well come along too just to have a look at that
crazy fellow's camp."   When they arrived at the
Little Mill, they beheld the meadows already
crowded with people, and Hampl's aide-de-camp
standing beside the two drums administering the
oath of allegiance to the Emperor Bobinet.   Here
and there bonfires were burning, with shadowy
figures flitting about them: in short, it all looked very
picturesque.   Several people went back to Hradec
visibly depressed.

By night the sight was even finer.   Skocdopole, the
Burgomaster, crept up the White Tower after midnight, and there to the east along the Orlice river
hundreds of fires were burning, thousands of figures

were moving about in the firelight, which cast a blood-red glow over the countryside. It looked as though entrenchments were being made. The Burgomaster came down from the tower deeply perturbed. It was evident that General Hampl's menaces regarding his military strength had not been exaggerated.

At dawn General Hampl emerged from the wooden mill, where he had sat up all night studying the plans of the city. Several thousand men, all of them in civilian clothes, but for the most part armed, had drawn themselves up in fours; women, old men, and children thronged around them.

"Forward," cried Hampl, and at the same instant the trumpets rang out in the brass band from Mr. Cerveny's world-famous wind-instrument works, and to the tune of a merry march ("The Girls along the Highway") Hampl's forces advanced upon the city.

General Hampl brought his troops to a halt before the city and sent forward a trumpeter and a herald with the demand that all non-combatants should leaves their houses. No one came out, however. The houses were empty.

The Little Square was empty.

The Great Square was empty.

The whole city was empty.

General Hampl twirled his moustache and made his way to City Hall. It was open. He entered the

Council Chamber. He took his seat in the Burgomaster's Chair. Sheets of paper were lying spread out in front of him on the green cloth, and on each of them these words had been written in a beautiful hand:

"In the name of His Majesty the Emperor Bobinet."

General Hampl stepped to the window and cried: "Soldiers, the battle is ended. You have crushed with the mailed fist the clerical tyranny of the Council clique. An era of progress and freedom has dawned for our beloved city. Return now, all of you, to your homes. You have played your part nobly. *Nazdar!*" ("Good luck go with you!")

"*Nazdar!*" responded the army, and dispersed.

One of Hampl's warriors (they came to be called simply Hampelmen) went back home to the Burgomaster's house; he had shouldered a rifle left behind by a Chinese soldier.

And so it was that Hampl became Mayor. It has to be acknowledged that amid the prevailing anarchy his prudent administration also was blessed with comparative peace, thanks to the wise counsels of Bishop Linda and the Worshipful City Fathers.

CHAPTER XXVII

A CORAL ISLAND IN THE PACIFIC

"WELL, I'll go to blazes," said Captain Trouble, "if that lanky fellow over there isn't their leader!"

"That's Jimmy," remarked G. H. Bondy. "He used to work here at one time. I thought he was quite tame by now."

"The devil must have owed me something," the Captain growled, "or I shouldn't have had to land here on this wretched . . . Hereheretua ! ! ! Eh?"

"Listen," said G. H. Bondy, laying his gun on the table on the veranda. "Is it the same as this in other places?"

"I should say so," boomed Captain Trouble. "Not far off, on Rawaiwai, Captain Barker and his whole crew were eaten. And on Mangai they had a banquet on three millionaires like yourself."

"Sutherland Bros.?" asked Bondy.

"I think so. And on Starbuck Island they roasted a High Commissioner. Is was that fat MacDeon; you know him, don't you?"

"No."

"You don't know him?" shouted the Captain. "How long have you been here, man?"

"This is my ninth year," said Mr. Bondy.

"Then you might well have known him," the Captain said. "So you've been here nine years? Business, eh? Or a little home of refuge, is it? On account of your nerves, I suppose?"

"No," said Mr. Bondy. "You see, I foresaw that they were all going to be at loggerheads over there, so I got out of the way. I thought that here I would find more peace."

"Aha, peace! You don't know our big black fellows! There's a bit of a war going on here all the time, my lad."

"Oh well," G. H. Bondy demurred, "there really was peace here. They're quite decent chaps, these Papuans or whatever you call them. It's only just recently that they've begun to be . . . rather disagreeable. I don't quite understand them. What are they really after?"

"Nothing special," said the Captain. "They only want to eat us."

"Are they as hungry as all that?" asked Bondy in amazement.

"I don't know. I think they do it more out of religion. It's one of their religious rites, don't you see? Something like communion, I take it. It takes them that way every now and then."

"Indeed," said Mr. Bondy thoughtfully.

"Everyone has his hobby," growled the Captain. "The local hobby here is to eat up the stranger and dry his head in smoke."

"What, smoke it as well?" Mr. Bondy exclaimed with horror.

"Oh, that's not done till after you're dead," said the Captain consolingly. "They cherish the smoked head as a souvenir. Have you ever seen those dried heads they've got in the Ethnographical Museum at Auckland?"

"No," said Bondy. "I don't think . . . that . . . that I'd look very attractive if I were smoked."

"You're a bit too fat for it," observed the Captain, inspecting him critically. "It doesn't make so very much difference to a thin man."

Bondy still looked anything but tranquil. He sat droopingly on the veranda of his bungalow on the coral island of Hereheretua, which he had purchased just before the outbreak of the Greatest War. Captain Trouble was glowering suspiciously at the thicket of mangroves and bananas which surrounded the bungalow.

"How many natives are there on the island?" he asked suddenly.

"About a hundred and twenty," said G. H. Bondy.

"And how many of us are there in the bungalow?"

"Seven, counting the Chinese cook."

The Captain sighed and looked out to sea. His ship, the *Papeete,* lay there at anchor; but to get to her he would have to go along a narrow path between the mangroves, and this did not precisely seem advisable.

"Look, here, sir," he said after a while, "what are they squabbling about over there, anyway? Some boundary or other?"

"Less than that."

"Colonies?"

"Even less than that."

"Commercial treaties?"

"No. Only about the truth."

"What kind of truth?"

"The absolute truth. You see, every nation insists that it has the absolute truth."

"Hm," grunted the Captain. "What is it, any-way?"

"Nothing. A sort of human passion. You've heard, haven't you, that in Europe yonder, and everywhere in fact, a . . . a God, you know . . . came into the world."

"Yes, I did hear that."

"Well, that's what it's all about, don't you under-stand?"

"No, I don't understand, old man. If you ask me, the true God would put things right in the world.

The one they've got can't be the true and proper God."

"On the contrary," said G. H. Bondy (obviously pleased at being able to talk for once with an independent and experienced human being), "I assure you that it *is* the true God. But I'll tell you something else. This true God is far too big."

"Do you think so?"

"I do indeed. He is infinite. That's just where the trouble lies. You see, everyone measures off a certain amount of Him and then thinks it is the entire God. Each one appropriates a little fringe or fragment of Him and then thinks he possesses the whole of Him. See?"

"Aha," said the Captain. "And then gets angry with everyone else who has a different bit of Him."

"Exactly. In order to convince himself that God is wholly his, he has to go and kill all the others. Just for that very reason, because it means so much to him to have the whole of God and the whole of the truth. That's why he can't bear anyone else to have any other God or any other truth. If he once allowed that, he would have to admit that he himself has only a few wretched metres or gallons or sackloads of divine truth. You see, suppose Dash were convinced that it was tremendously important that only Dash's underwear should be the best on earth, he would have to burn his rival, Blank, and all

Blank's underwear. But Dash isn't so silly as that in the matter of underwear; he is only as silly as that in the matter of religion or English politics. If he believed that God was something as substantial and essential as underwear, he would allow other people to provide themselves with Him just as they pleased. But he hasn't sufficient commercial confidence in Him; and so he forces Dash's God or Dash's Truth on everybody with curses, wars and other unreliable forms of advertisement. I am a business man and I understand competition, but this sort of . . ."

"Wait a minute," interrupted Captain Trouble, and aimed a shot into the mangrove thicket. "There, I think that's one less of them."

"He died for his faith," whispered Bondy dreamily. "You have forcibly restrained him from devouring me. He fell for the national ideal of cannibalism. In Europe people have been devouring each other from time immemorial out of idealism. You are a decent man, Captain, but it's quite possible that you'd devour me on behalf of any fundamental principle of navigation. I've lost confidence even in you."

"You're quite right," the Captain grumbled. "When I look at you, I feel that I'm . . ."

". . . . a violent anti-Semite. I know. That doesn't matter, I had myself baptized. But do you know, Captain, what's got hold of those black idiots?

The night before last they fished out of the sea a Japanese atomic torpedo. They've set it up over there under the coco-nut palms, and now they are bowing down before it. Now they have a God of their own. That's why they must devour us."

War-cries sounded from the mangrove thicket.

"Do you hear them?" muttered the Captain. "On my soul, I'd rather . . . go through the geometry examination all over again. . . ."

"Listen," Bondy whispered. "Couldn't we go over to their religion? As far as I am concerned . . ."

At that moment a gun boomed out from the *Papeete*.

The Captain uttered a low cry of joy.

CHAPTER XXVIII

AT SEVEN COTTAGES

A<small>ND</small> while the world shook with the clash of armies, while the boundaries of States writhed to and fro like earth-worms, and the whole earth was crumbling into a field of ruins, old Mrs. Blahous was peeling her potatoes in Seven Cottages, Grandfather Blahous was sitting on the doorstep smoking beech-leaves, and their neighbour, Mrs. Prouzova, was leaning on the fence, repeating meditatively, "Yes, yes."

"Aye, yes," returned Blahous after a while.

"My word, yes," observed Mrs. Blahous.

"That's how 'tis," Mrs. Prouzova answered.

"Oh, what's the use?" said Grandfather Blahous.

"Yes, that's it," added Mrs. Blahous, peeling another potato.

"They say the Italians got a good hiding," Blahous announced.

"Who from?"

"From the Turks, I expect."

"Then, I suppose that'll be the end of the war?"

"What d'you mean? The Prussians 'll start off now."

"What, against us?"

"Against the French, they say."

"Good heavens above, everything will be dear again."

"Yes, yes."

"Aye, yes."

"What's the use?"

"They say that the Swiss wrote not long ago that the others might give it up soon."

"That's what I say."

"Yes. Why, the day before yesterday I paid fifteen hundred crowns for a candle. I tell you, Blahous, it was one of those miserable things only fit for the stable."

"And you mean to say it cost you fifteen hundred?"

"Not far off. There's a rise for you, friends!"

"Aye, yes."

"My word, yes."

"Who's ever have thought it? Fifteen hundred!"

"You could get a fine candle for two hundred at one time."

"Yes, auntie, but that's years ago. Why, even an egg only cost five hundred in those days."

"And you could get a pound of butter for three thousand."

"And lovely butter, too!"

"And boots for eight thousand."

"Yes, yes, Mrs. Blahous, things were cheap in those days."

"But now——"

"Yes, yes."

"If only it was all over and done with!"

There was silence. Old Blahous rose, straightened his back, and went into the yard for a wisp of straw.

"Oh, what's the use?" he said, unscrewing the head of his pipe in order to pull the straw through.

"It wasn't half smelling before," remarked Mrs. Blahous, full of interest.

"Smelling," said Blahous, nodding. "How can it help smelling? There's no tobacco left in the world now. The last packet I had was the one my son the Professor sent me—let me see, that was in '49, wasn't it?"

"That was just four years ago come Easter."

"So 'twas," said Granfather Blahous. "We're getting an old man now. Very, very old."

"And what I want to know," began Mrs. Prouzova, "is what's all this awful to-do about nowadays?"

"What to-do?"

"Well, this war, I mean."

"Aye, yes, Heaven knows what it's about," said Blahous, blowing down his pipe until it gurgled.

"That's what nobody knows, aunt. They say it's about religion—that's what they tell me."

"What sort of religion?"

"Oh, ours or the Swiss—nobody knows which. It's so as there'll be only one religion, they say."

"Well, we used to have only one religion before."

"But other places had a different one, aunt. They say there was orders from above that there must be only one."

"What sort of orders? Where from?"

"Nobody knows. They say there were once machines that had religion inside of them. It was hidden in a sort of long boiler."

"And what were the boilers for?"

"Nobody knows. Just a sort of boilers. And they say that God appeared to people to make them believe. There was a lot in those days, aunt, that didn't believe. One has to believe in something; what's the use? If people had only believed, God wouldn't have appeared to them. So it was only their godlessness that made Him come into the world, see, aunt?"

"Well, yes, but what did this awful war begin for?"

"Nobody knows. People say that the Chinese or the Turks began it. They say that they brought their own God with them in those boilers. They're supposed to be terrible religious, the Turks and the

Chinese. And so they wanted us to believe the way they did."

"But why should we?"

"That's it, nobody knows. If you ask me, the Prussians started it. And the Swedes, too."

"Lord, Lord!" lamented Mrs. Prouzova. "And the prices things are now! Fifteen hundred for a candle!"

"And what I say," maintained old Blahous, "is the Jews started the war so as to make money out of it. That's what I say."

"We could do with some rain," observed Mrs. Blahous. "The potatoes are far too small. Like nuts."

"It's my belief," Blahous went on, "that people just invented that about the Lord God, so as to have someone to blame things on. That was all made up. They wanted a war and they wanted an excuse. It was all a put-up job."

"Who did it, then?"

"Nobody knows. What I say is, it was all fixed up with the Pope and the Jews and the whole lot of them. Those . . . those . . . KALBURATORS!" shouted Grandfather Blahous, in great excitement. "I'd like to say it to their faces! Why, did anybody need a new Lord God? The old one was good enough for us country people. There was just enough of Him, and He was good, and honest and upright. He didn't show himself to anybody, but we had peace instead. . . ."

"What are you asking for your eggs, Prouzova?"

"I'm getting two thousand each at present."

"They say they're asking three in Trutnov."

"And I tell you," declared old Blahous vehemently, "it was bound to come. People were cross with each other even then. Why, your husband that's dead now, Prouzova, God rest his soul, was a spiritualist or medium or something in those days. And one time I said to him just in fun, 'I say, Prouza, you might call back that evil spirit that's just escaped from me.' And he lost his temper, and from that day to the day of his death he never spoke a word to me again. Yet he was my neighbour, mind you, aunt. And look at Tony Vlcek. He always swore by those foxfates that you fertilize with, and if anyone didn't believe in them, he'd keep on going for him like mad. And my son, the Professor, tells me it's the same wherever you go. If anyone sets his mind on anything, he must have everybody else believe in it. And he won't let anyone alone. That's how it's all come about."

"Yes, yes," said Aunt Prouzova, yawning. "What's the use of it all?"

"Ah, yes," sighed Mrs. Blahous.

"That's the way things are in this world," added Mrs. Prouzova.

"And you women would like to go on cackling all day long," Grandfather Blahous concluded peevishly, and tottered off into the house.

. . . And the earth shook with the clash of armies, and thinkers in every camp confidently asserted that "a brighter day was dawning."

CHAPTER XXIX

THE LAST BATTLE

IN the autumn of 1953 the Greatest War was drawing to a close. There were no armies left. The
armies of occupation, cut off for the most part from
their homes, were dwindling away and gradually
vanishing like water in the sand. Self-appointed
generals marched from town to town, or rather from
heap to heap of ruins, at the head of five men, one
a drummer, one a thief, one a schoolboy, one a man
with a gramophone, and one of whom nobody knew
anything. They went about collecting contributions
or arranging benefit performances "in aid of the
wounded and their widows and orphans." No one
knew by now how many warring camps there were.

Amid this universal and indescribable collapse
the Greatest War drew to its close. The end came
so unexpectedly that no one nowadays can tell just
where the last so-called decisive battle was fought.
Historians are still at variance as to which engage-
ment marked the close and extinction of the world-
conflagration. Certain of them (such as Dührich,
Assbridge, and more particularly Moroni) are

inclined to the view that it was the battle of Lintz. In these extensive operations sixty soldiers were engaged, representing eleven hostile camps. The conflict broke out in the large saloon of the Rose Inn, the immediate cause being the waitress Hilda (as a matter of fact it was Marena Ruzickova of Novy Bydzov). Giuseppe, the Italian, proved victorious and carried Hilda off; but since she ran away next day with a Czech called Vaclav Hruska, this too was not a decisive battle.

The historian Usinski records a similar battle at Gorochovky, Leblond a skirmish at Le Batignolles, and Van Goo a fight near Nieuport; but it would seem that local patriotism influenced them more directly than genuinely historical motives. In short, no one knows which was the last battle of the Greatest War. Nevertheless, it can be determined with considerable certitude from documents that are striking in their agreement, i.e. the series of prophecies that appeared before the Greatest War.

For example, a phophecy printed in Swabian characters had been preserved since 1845, foretelling that in a hundred years "terrible times will come, and many armed men will fall in battle," but that "in a hundred months *thirteen* nations would meet in the field *under a birch-tree,* and slaughter each other in a desperate struggle," which would be followed by fifty years of peace.

In the year 1893 the Turkish prophetess Wali Schön (?) predicted that "five times twelve years would pass ere peace would reign over the whole world; in that year *thirteen* emperors would make war upon each other and would meet in battle *under a birch-tree.* Then there would be peace, such a peace as there had never been before and never would be again."

The vision of a certain negress in Massachusetts is also quoted, dating from 1909, when she beheld "a black monster with two horns, a yellow monster with three horns, and a red monster with eight horns, fighting *under a tree* (birch-tree?) until their blood besprinkled the whole world." It is interesting to note that the total number of horns is thirteen, apparently symbolical of the thirteen nations.

In 1920 the Very Reverend Dr. Arnold foretold that "there would be a great Twenty Years' War in which the whole world would be involved. One great Emperor would perish in that war, three great Empires would fall, ninety-nine capital cities would be destroyed, and the last battle of that war would be the last battle of the century."

To the same year belong "The Vision of Jonathan" (printed in Stockholm): "War and pestilence will lay waste nine-and-ninety countries, and nine-and-ninety kingdoms will vanish and rise again. The last battle will last nine-and-ninety hours, and will be so bloody that all the victors will be able to find room in the shade of one *birch-tree.*"

A German popular prophecy dating from 1923 speaks of the battle on the Birkenfeld (*Birch field*).

More than two hundred similar prophetic documents of the period between 1845 and 1944 have been preserved. In forty-eight of these the number "thirteen" occurs; in seventy of them the "birch-tree" appears; in fifteen merely the "tree." It may therefore be concluded that the last battle took place in the neighbourhood of a birch-tree. Who took part in the struggle we do not know, but there were altogether only thirteen men left alive out of the various armies, and they presumably lay down after the battle in the shade of a birch-tree. That moment saw the end of the Greatest War.

It is, however, possible that the "birch" is brought in symbolically, instead of a place-name. There are one hundred and seven places in the country of the Czechs alone containing the Czech word for birch, such as Brezany, Brezovice, and Brezolupy. Then there is the German *Birke* and names like Birkenberg, Birkenfeld, Birkenhaid, Birkenhammer, Birkicht, Birkental, etc.; or the English Birkenhead, Birchington, Birchanger, and so on; or the French Boulainvilliers, Boulay, etc. Thus the number of towns, villages, and localities where the last battle in all probability took place is narrowed down to a few thousand (as long as we confine ourselves to Europe, which certainly has a prior claim to the Last Battle). Individual scientific research will establish where it occurred. Who won it cannot possibly be determined.

But perhaps after all—the fancy is alluring—there did stand near the scene of the last act of the world-tragedy a slender silvery birch. Perhaps a lark sang above the battle-field and a white butterfly fluttered over the heads of the combatants. And look, by this time there is hardly anyone left to kill! It is a hot October day, and one hero after another steps aside, turns his back upon the battle-field, eases himself, and lies down longing for peace in the shadow of the birch-tree. At last the whole thirteen of them are lying there, all the survivors of the Last Battle. One lays his weary head on his neighbour's boots, another rests his on the first man's back, undisturbed by his breathing. The last thirteen soldiers left in the world as asleep beneath a birch-tree.

Towards evening they waken, look at each other with suspicion, and reach for their weapons. And then one of them—history will never learn his name—says, "Oh, damn it, boys, let's chuck it!"

"Right you are, mate," says the second man with relief, laying aside his weapon.

"Give us a bit of bacon, then, fathead," the third one asks with a certain gentleness.

The fourth man returns, "Crikey, I could do with a smoke. Hasn't anybody got a——?"

"Let's clear off, boys," urges the fifth. "We're not going to have any more of it."

"I'll give you a cigarette," says the sixth, "but you'll have to give me a bit of bread."

"We're going home, boys . . . think of it . . . home," the seventh one cries.

"Is your old woman expecting you?" the eighth man asks.

"My God, it's six years since I slept in a proper bed," sighs the ninth.

"What a mug's game it was, lads!" says the tenth man, spitting disgustedly.

"It was that!" the eleventh replies, "but we've done with it now."

"We've done with it," repeats the twelfth man. "We're not such fools. Let's go home, mates!"

"Oh, but I'm glad it's all over," concludes the thirteenth, turning over to lie on the other side.

And such, one can well imagine, was the end of the Greatest War.

CHAPTER XXX

THE END OF EVERYTHING

MANY years went by. Brych the stoker, now the proprietor of a locksmith's business, was sitting in the Damohorsky tavern, reading a copy of the *People's Journal.*

"The liver sausages will be ready in a minute," announced the landlord, emerging from the kitchen. And bless me if it wasn't old Jan Binder, who used to own the merry-go-round. He had grown fat and no longer wore his striped jersey; nevertheless it was he!

"There's no hurry," Mr. Brych answered slowly. "Father Jost hasn't turned up yet. Nor Rejzek either."

"And—how is Mr. Kuzenda getting along?" Jan Binder inquired.

"Oh, well, you know. He's not very grand. He's one of the best men breathing, Mr. Binder."

"He is, indeed," assented the innkeeper. "I don't know . . . Mr. Brych . . . what about taking him a few liver saugages with my compliments? They're first class, Mr. Brych, and if you'd be so kind . . ."

"Why, with pleasure, Mr. Binder. He'll be delighted to think you remember him. Of course I will. With pleasure!"

"Praise be the Lord!" came a voice from the doorway, and Canon Jost stepped into the room, his cheeks ruddy with the cold, and hung up his hat and fur coat.

"Good evening, your Reverence," responded Mr. Brych. "We've waited for you—we've waited."

Father Jost pursed his lips contentedly and rubbed his stiffened hands. "Well, sir, what's in the papers, what have they got to say to-day?"

"I was just reading this: 'The President of the Republic has appointed that youthful savant, Dr. Blahous, Lecturer at the University, to be Assistant Professor.' You remember, Canon, it's that Blahous who once wrote an article about Mr. Kuzenda."

"Aha, aha," said Father Jost, wiping his little spectacles. "I know, I know, the atheist. They are a lot of infidels at the University. And you're another, Mr. Brych."

"Come, his Reverence will pray for us, I know," said Mr. Binder. "He'll want us in heaven to make up the card-party. Well, your Reverence, two and one?"

"Yes, of course, two and one."

Mr. Binder opened the kitchen door and shouted:

"Two liver sausages and one blood-sausage."

" 'Evening!" growled Rejzek, the journalist, entering the room. "It's cold, friends."

"It's a very pleasant evening," chirped Mr. Binder. "We don't get company like this every day."

"Well, what's the news?" inquired Father Jost gaily. "What's going on in the editorial sanctum? Ah, yes, I used to write for the papers myself in my young days."

"By the way, that fellow Blahous mentioned me in the paper too that time," said Mr. Brych. "I've still go the cutting somewhere: 'The Apostle of Kuzenda's Sect,' or something like that, he called me. Yes, yes, those were the days!"

"Let's have supper," ordered Mr. Rejzek. Mr. Binder and his daughter were already setting sausages on the table. They were still sizzling, covered with frothing bubbles of fat, and they reclined upon crisp sauerkraut like Turkish odalisques on cushions. Father Jost clicked his tongue resoundingly and cut into the first beauty before him.

"Splendid," said Mr. Brych after a while.

"Mhm," came from Mr. Rejzek after a lengthier interval.

"Binder, these do you credit," said the Canon approvingly.

A silence ensued, full of appreciation and pious meditations.

"Allspice," contributed Mr. Brych. "I love the smell of it."

"But it mustn't be too much in evidence."

"No, this is just as it should be."

"And the skin must be just crisp enough."

"Mhm." And again conversation ceased for a space.

"And the sauerkraut must be nice and white."

"In Moravia," said Mr. Brych, "they make the sauerkraut like a sort of porridge. I was there as an apprentice. It's quite runny."

"Oh, come," exclaimed Father Jost. "Sauerkraut has to be strained. Don't talk such nonsense. Why, the stuff wouldn't be fit to eat."

"Well, there you are . . . they do eat it that way down there. With spoons."

"Horrible!" cried the Canon, marvelling. "What extraordinary people they must be, friends! Why, sauerkraut should only just be greased, shouldn't it, Mr. Binder? I don't understand how anyone could have it any other way."

"Well, you know," said Mr. Brych meditatively, "it's just the same with sauerkraut as it is with religion. One man can't understand how another can believe anything different."

"Oh, enough of that!" protested Father Jost. "Why, I'd sooner believe in Mahomet than eat sauerkraut made any other way. After all, reason teaches one that sauerkraut ought only to be greased."

"And don't reason teach one one's religion."

"Our religion, certainly," said the Canon decisively. "But the others are not based on reason."

"Now we've got back again to just where we were before the war," sighed Mr. Brych.

"People are always getting back just where they used to be," observed Mr. Binder. "That's what Mr. Kuzenda is always saying. 'Binder,' he often says, 'the truth can never be defeated. You know, Binder,' he says, 'that God of ours on the dredge in those days wasn't so bad, nor was yours on the merry-go-round, and yet, you see, they've both of them vanished. Everyone believes in his own superior God, but he doesn't believe in another man, or credit him with believing in something good. People should first of all believe in other people, and the rest would soon follow.' That's what Mr. Kuzenda always says."

"Yes, yes," assented Mr. Brych. "A man may certainly think that another religion is a bad one, but he oughtn't to think that the man who follows it is a low, vile, and treacherous fellow. And the same applies to politics and everything."

"And that's what so many people have hated and killed each other for," Father Jost declared. "You know, the greater the things are in which a man believes, the more fiercely he despises those who do not believe in them. And yet the greatest of all beliefs would be belief in one's fellow-men."

"Everyone has the best of feelings towards mankind in general, but not towards the individual man. We'll kill men, but we want to save mankind. And that isn't right, your Reverence. The world will be an evil place as long as people don't believe in other people."

"Mr. Binder," said Father Jost thoughtfully, "I wonder if you would make me some of that Moravian sauerkraut to-morrow. I'd like to try it."

"It has to be partly stewed and then steamed, and done like that with a fried sausage it's very good. Every religion and every truth has something good in it, if it's only the fact that it suits somebody else."

The door was opened from outside, and a policeman stepped in. He was chilled to the bone and wanted a glass of rum.

"Ah, it's you, is it, Sergeant Hruska," said Brych. "Well now, where have you come from?"

"Oh, we've been up in Zizkov," answered the policeman, pulling off his enormous gloves. "There was a raid on."

"What did you catch?"

"Oh, a couple of roughs, and a few undesirables. And then at number 1006—in the cellar of the house, I mean—there was a den."

"What sort of den?" inquired Mr. Rejzek.

"A Karburator den, sir. They had set up a tiny Karburator down there out of an old pre-war motor. A very low crowd has been going down there and holding orgies."

"What kind of orgies do you mean?"

"Oh, disorderly behaviour. They pray and sing and have visions and prophesy and perform miracles, and all that sort of business."

"And isn't that allowed?"

"No, it's forbidden by the police. You see, it's something like those dens where they smoke opium. We found one of them in the Old Town. We've routed out seven of these Karburator caverns already. An awful gang used to collect there: vagrants, loose women, and other doubtful characters. That's why it's forbidden. It's a breach of the peace."

"And are there many haunts of this kind?"

"Not now. I think this one was the last of the Karburators."

In the Bison Frontiers of Imagination series

Tarzan Alive
By Philip José Farmer
New foreword by Win Scott Eckert
Introduced by Mike Resnick

The Circus of Dr. Lao
By Charles G. Finney
Introduced by John Marco

Omega: The Last Days of the World
By Camille Flammarion
Introduced by Robert Silverberg

Ralph 124C 41+
By Hugo Gernsback
Introduced by Jack Williamson

*The Journey of Niels Klim to
the World Underground*
By Ludvig Holberg
Introduced and edited by
James I. McNelis Jr.
Preface by Peter Fitting

The Lost Continent: The Story of Atlantis
By C. J. Cutcliffe Hyne
Introduced by Harry Turtledove
Afterword by Gary Hoppenstand

*The Great Romance:
A Rediscovered Utopian Adventure*
By The Inhabitant
Edited by Dominic Alessio

Mizora: A World of Women
By Mary E. Bradley Lane
Introduced by Joan Saberhagen

A Voyage to Arcturus
By David Lindsay
Introduced by John Clute

Before Adam
By Jack London
Introduced by Dennis L. McKiernan

Fantastic Tales
By Jack London
Edited by Dale L. Walker

*Master of Adventure:
The Worlds of Edgar Rice Burroughs*
By Richard A. Lupoff
With an introduction to the Bison
Books Edition by the author
Foreword by Michael Moorcock
Preface by Henry Hardy Heins
With an essay by Phillip R. Burger

The Moon Pool
By A. Merritt
Introduced by Robert Silverberg

The Purple Cloud
By M. P. Shiel
Introduced by John Clute

Shadrach in the Furnace
By Robert Silverberg

Lost Worlds
By Clark Ashton Smith
Introduced by Jeff VanderMeer

Out of Space and Time
By Clark Ashton Smith
Introduced by Jeff VanderMeer

The Skylark of Space
By E. E. "Doc" Smith
Introduced by Vernor Vinge

Skylark Three
By E. E. "Doc" Smith
Introduced by Jack Williamson

*The Nightmare and Other Tales
of Dark Fantasy*
By Francis Stevens
Edited and introduced by
Gary Hoppenstand

Tales of Wonder
By Mark Twain
Edited, introduced, and with
notes by David Ketterer

The Chase of the Golden Meteor
By Jules Verne
Introduced by Gregory A. Benford

*The Golden Volcano: The First English
Translation of Verne's Original Manuscript*
By Jules Verne
Translated and edited by Edward Baxter

*Lighthouse at the End of the World:
The First English Translation of Verne's
Original Manuscript*
By Jules Verne
Translated and edited by William Butcher

*The Meteor Hunt: The First English
Translation of Verne's Original Manuscript*
By Jules Verne
Translated and edited by Frederick Paul
Walter and Walter James Miller

The Croquet Player
By H. G. Wells
Afterword by John Huntington

In the Days of the Comet
By H. G. Wells
Introduced by Ben Bova

The Last War: A World Set Free
By H. G. Wells
Introduced by Greg Bear

The Sleeper Awakes
By H. G. Wells
Introduced by J. Gregory Keyes
Afterword by Gareth Davies-Morris

The War in the Air
By H. G. Wells
Introduced by Dave Duncan

The Disappearance
By Philip Wylie
Introduced by Robert Silverberg

Gladiator
By Philip Wylie
Introduced by Janny Wurts

When Worlds Collide
By Philip Wylie and Edwin Balmer
Introduced by John Varley

To order or obtain more information on these or other University of Nebraska Press titles, visit www.nebraskapress.unl.edu.

9 780803 264595